WHISTLING
IN THE DARK

The War Brides Trilogy:
Book Two

Other books by Amanda Harte:

The *War Brides* Trilogy:
Dancing in the Rain

The *Unwanted Legacies* Series:
Imperfect Together
Strings Attached

Moonlight Masquerade

WHISTLING
IN THE DARK

•

Amanda Harte

AVALON BOOKS
NEW YORK

PRINTED IN THE UNITED STATES OF AMERICA
ON ACID-FREE PAPER
BY HADDON CRAFTSMEN, BLOOMSBURG, PENNSYLVANIA

For Deborrah Darroch,
whose letters have brightened so many days.
Thanks, Debbie.

Chapter One

Calais, France, May 1918

It wasn't supposed to be this difficult. Emily Wentworth placed a wrench on the bolt and tightened it. That was simple. If only everything else were! She, the woman who was known for her ability to see the silver lining in the darkest of clouds, was finding it increasingly difficult to discover anything positive about her current situation.

Her boot heels clicked on the cobblestones, and not for the first time Emily was struck by how greatly her life had changed in less than three months. If it hadn't been for the telegram, she would be home in Canela, where it was warm and dry. Instead, she was thousands of miles away in northern France, where warm, dry days were a rarity.

Emily didn't mind the cold; her boots kept the worst of it from her feet and ankles. High-button boots and woollen skirts might not be fashionable, but fashion counted for little here. What mattered was saving lives. She wouldn't even mind the rain, if it weren't for the fact that rain created mud, and muddy roads were difficult to traverse. What she minded were the delays.

As Emily reached down for the oil can, a lock of hair escaped from her chignon and bounced against her cheek. Impatiently she tucked the loose hair behind her ear. Perhaps she should have taken her sisters' advice and bobbed her hair. At the time, she had thought that long hair would be easier to care for; now she wasn't so certain. At this point, she wasn't certain of much other than the fact that she could not fail.

Emily looked at the building where she spent so much of her time. In happier times it had been a stable, housing the horses and grand carriages that transported the duke and duchess who lived in the chateau. Those happier times had ended almost four years earlier, when war had first been declared. The duke had volunteered his home as a hospital, and the stable had been converted to a garage. Instead of horses with proud bloodlines, it now housed two automobiles whose long bodies and bright red crosses left no doubt of their function. The duke had done his part. Emily would too. But first she had to prove that the Army was wrong.

She had thought the most difficult challenge would be talking her way into the war that everyone was calling the War to End All Wars. Despite her sisters' claims that she couldn't, it had proven surprisingly easy. When the officials had learned that Emily could not only drive but also repair an automobile, they had been eager to send her to France. Ambulance drivers, they had confirmed, were in short supply, and women who understood the difference between a connecting rod and a magneto were in even shorter supply.

The bureaucrats, far from putting obstacles in her way, had quickly agreed to let her sail on the next ship. Of course, they hadn't known the real reason Emily was anxious to go to France. If they had . . . Emily frowned. She hadn't lied. That much was true. She wouldn't dwell on the half truths that she had told, for they had been necessary, and without them, she doubted anyone would have let her cross the ocean.

The actual sea voyage had been easier than she had expected. Because the winter storms had ended, crossing the Atlantic had been literally smooth sailing. It was only after she landed that things became difficult. Though it had taken just short of a month to travel the 4,000 miles from Texas to France, in the last month, she had gotten not one mile—not even an inch—closer to her destination. Emily Wentworth was stuck in Calais, and that most definitely was not where she wanted to be.

She stood, straightening her back and rolling her shoulders as she tried to ease the kink in them. It was early afternoon, the time of the day when the elderly Frenchmen who normally bustled about the courtyard returned home to dine with their families. Today Emily had foregone dinner, knowing that the ambulance needed to be repaired before the evening train of wounded arrived. Gertie, as the staff at the hospital had nicknamed this ambulance, was notably temperamental, and repairs sometimes took the whole day. That was the reason Emily had remained in the converted stable.

She took a deep breath, marveling not for the first time at the fact that the smells of gasoline and oil, strong as they were, failed to mask the odors of the animals that had lived here for centuries. Though the walls between the stalls had been removed to provide room for the hospital's two ambulances, there was no denying that this was a stable, not a garage.

Emily glanced outside. Judging from the length of the shadows, the midday break was almost over. That meant that she had been in here for five hours. She winced as she stretched her muscles. Though she enjoyed working on Henry Ford's marvelous creations almost as much as she did driving them, there was no denying the fact that leaning over a motor for hours at a time could be a painful experience. Theo used to say . . .

Emily closed her eyes as she fought back a wave of anguish. How selfish of her to think about a sore back when thousands of men were living in trenches, enduring unspeakable conditions to make the world safe again. She couldn't forget them, any more than she could forget the reason she had traveled so far and practiced so much deception. Though Martha had warned her of the impossibility of her mission and Carolyn had insisted she would find only heartbreak, Emily had refused to listen to her sisters. They were wrong, just as the men who had sent that horrible telegram were wrong. She would prove it to them all. She would not fail, any more than she would believe what they said about Theo.

At the sound of footsteps on the cobblestones, Emily opened her eyes and fixed a smile on her face. Sarah Gilmore, the petite brunette from Kansas who had welcomed Emily the day her ship docked, was approaching and, if the basket she had slung over one arm was any indication, she was bringing food.

"When I didn't see you at dinner, I figured you were having a hard time with Gertie."

As Sarah opened the top of the basket, delicious aromas wafted into the warm spring air, mingling with the scents of new leaves and the perfume of the few hyacinths that had survived the conversion of the elegant three-story stone building from residence to hospital. At one time, Emily had been told, the central courtyard had been filled with flowers. That time was long gone. The constant stream of pedestrians had turned grass to mud, and now only a few hardy spring bulbs remained.

"Hungry?" Sarah asked.

"As a horse."

Emily closed the tool box. There were no chairs in the

garage, but the tool box was large enough to serve as a bench. She took a bite of the baguette Sarah had spread with pâté and savored the flavors. Though wartime had limited the availability of fresh ingredients, Emily marveled at their cook's skill. Who would have thought that chopped liver served on crusty bread would taste so good? In his own way, the elderly chef was part of the war effort. Emily was, too, or she would be, if only . . .

"You were frowning when I came in, and you almost never frown." Sarah patted the vehicle's front fender. "Is something wrong with Gertie?"

Emily shook her head. "The ambulance is fine," she told her friend. "Don't worry. We'll be able to meet the train this afternoon." Like Emily's sister Carolyn, Sarah was a nurse and, because her bedside manner was so reassuring, she was often assigned to the ambulance corps. It was an arrangement Emily liked, for she enjoyed working with Sarah. The brunette's infectious laughter made the wounded men relax, and that helped Emily, for when they were relaxed, ruts in the road didn't seem so deep and the men did not cry out in pain.

"If Gertie is fine," Sarah said, "why were you frowning?"

Emily took another bite of bread, then chewed slowly as she decided how to respond. "I think they call it cabin fever. The sun is finally shining. The roads are starting to dry, and I'm feeling a bit trapped here in Calais." That was an understatement, but it was all Emily would say. She couldn't let anyone know why she was here, not when so much depended on people believing that she was just another American whose sense of duty had led her to join the glorious cause.

Emily took a spoonful of the apple compote Sarah had brought her, enjoying the light spices that enhanced the fruit's flavor. "When I volunteered to be an ambulance driver, I thought I'd be closer to the front." And closer to

Theo. He was alive, and he needed her. Emily knew that as surely as she knew that the sun was past its zenith. Theo was somewhere here in France, waiting for her to find him.

"Most of the drivers do get sent to the front." Sarah began to repack the basket as she confirmed what Emily had heard. "I suspect they're keeping you here because you're so good at repairing the ambulances. I overheard one of the officers say he'd never seen anyone with your skill."

Emily took a sip of water. Though she wasn't thirsty, the glass helped camouflage her reaction to Sarah's words. So that was why she remained here! Had she known that being able to tighten bolts and replace tires would be a liability rather than an asset, Emily would never have admitted her expertise. She would have counted on the War Department's need for ambulance drivers being enough to get her shipped to France.

Apparently oblivious to Emily's distress, Sarah sat on the tool chest, swinging her legs as if she had not a worry in the world. "Who taught you to fix motor cars?" she asked.

"My brother." The words slipped out before Emily had a chance to think. Now, like the contents of Pandora's box, they were out in the open.

"Your brother?" Sarah raised a carefully groomed eyebrow. "I didn't know you had one. You've spoken of your sisters, but you never mentioned a brother."

There was a good reason for that. In the eyes of the world, Emily no longer had a brother. "Theo's dead. He was killed somewhere on the Western Front." It hurt, oh, how it hurt to pronounce those words. They weren't true; she wouldn't believe they were true, but still . . .

Sarah put her arms around Emily and hugged her. "I don't know what to say," she confessed. " 'I'm sorry' seems so inadequate. Is there anything I can do to help you?"

"Talk about something—anything—that won't remind me of Theo."

It was all the encouragement Sarah needed. For the next few minutes, she regaled Emily with tales of the handsome doctor who had been assigned to their hospital, while Emily began to oil the brake cam.

"It sounds as if Dr. Mercer has been sweet talking you," Emily said when Sarah paused to take a breath. Their sister Carolyn had attracted beaux the way a pot of honey attracted bees, a fact that Emily and Theo had found so amusing that they would bring out a jar of honey and offer it to the unsuspecting young swain. Though Carolyn had not been amused, Emily and Theo would roar with laughter at the young men's discomfit. *Stop it!* Emily admonished herself. *Stop thinking of Theo.* But that was impossible when she knew that her twin needed her.

Oblivious to the direction Emily's thoughts had strayed, Sarah blushed and said, "Fred's got a way with words, no doubt about it, but when it comes to words, he can't compare to Grant Randall. No one can."

Though Emily thought for a moment, she could not recall anyone at the hospital being named Grant Randall. "Who's he?" she asked.

Her question appeared to startle Sarah, for the brunette's voice held a note of incredulity. "I don't believe it. You've been in France for a month and you haven't read Grant Randall's column. That must be a record."

Emily moved to the other side of the ambulance to oil the other rear brake. "Grant Randall is a writer?"

"He's not just a writer," Sarah said, her voice mildly outraged. "He's one of the best war correspondents we have."

Emily straightened and moved toward the vehicle's front.

"That explains why I haven't heard of him. I haven't read a newspaper since I arrived." She hadn't wanted to. Now that she was thousands of miles closer to Theo, she hadn't wanted to follow the day-to-day reports of the war and the devastation that it was bringing to Europe. It might be an ostrich-in-the-sand attitude, but she didn't want to think about the families whose lives would never be the same. All she wanted was to find her brother.

"You need to hear what Grant Randall has to say. Wait right here." Emily smiled as Sarah hurried toward the stone building that they now called home. It wasn't as if Emily had any choices. She had to remain here. That was the problem.

When Sarah returned, she was brandishing a piece of newsprint. "Listen to this," she said, and began to read.

Though she didn't want to hear about the war, Emily could not close her ears, and by the time Sarah finished, she was dashing tears from her eyes. "It's beautiful," she said softly. "He's describing something truly horrible— men living in the trenches, dealing with seemingly sense- less death—and yet he manages to turn it into something noble."

Emily replaced the oil tin and picked up a can of gaso- line. Fueling the car was her last task before she test drove it. She moved almost as mechanically as the ambulance, but her thoughts were in a whirl. Though she hadn't ex- pected it, Grant Randall's words had brought her closer to her brother. For the first time Emily understood why Theo had written that he wouldn't have traded his wartime ex- periences for anything. At the time she had been hurt. Until he volunteered for the war, they had never been separated. When Theo had announced that he was joining the Army, Emily had feared the loss of the closeness—that special connection—they had always shared, and his letters, de- scribing life in the trenches and the camaraderie that had developed with the other Doughboys, had left her feeling oddly excluded. Now Emily understood that Theo, like Grant Randall, had been searching for something positive, some redeeming aspect to an otherwise horrendous experience. She should have realized that Theo had been following her lead, playing the game she had initiated when they were children, the game of looking for a silver lining.

If only she could find one now! Emily bit the inside of her cheek, trying to keep her fears at bay. The telegram was a huge mistake. She wouldn't—couldn't—believe anything else, for the alternative was too painful to consider. Theo was not dead. Emily was positive that he had survived the brutal attack on his battalion. Though the Army and her sisters believed otherwise, Emily knew her brother was alive.

She took a deep breath and let it out slowly in a vain attempt to quell her sense that nothing would ever again be right. Somehow, someway, she would find Theo. It might not be easy, but she would learn where her brother was, and then she would devise a way to reach him. She had to.

"I'm sorry, sir. It won't go."

Grant Randall climbed out of the black monstrosity and glared at it. There was no point in being annoyed with Robert. The man did his best under difficult conditions. But the hulk of metal that was now blocking the roadway was a different story. "Whoever called Henry Ford a genius hasn't spent much time in one of these contraptions."

"No, sir."

They were a mere 20 miles from their destination, but at the rate they were going, they would not reach Calais before nightfall. Grant pulled out his watch and shook his head in disgust. "This is an abomination. It's only been an hour since the last problem." He had thought that once they left the front, the hazards would be behind them. While it was true that the enemy was not shelling this road and that, if a man didn't look too closely at the farms they were passing, he could pretend that this part of France had not been bombed, traversing the narrow tree-lined road had proven to be far more difficult than he had anticipated.

Grant didn't mind the ruts. They were the inevitable result of the heavy spring rains. Instead, he focused on the fact that the road was beginning to dry and that the mechanical beast had not gotten stuck in the mire even a single time. But that appeared to be the only mishap that had not befallen his transport.

The first time the automobile had sputtered to a stop, Grant had been philosophical. Everything, he told himself, was grist for a writer's mill. He would take mental notes of his surroundings, for who knew when he might be able to contrast the apparently tranquil country road, whose stately poplars had begun to leaf out, with the rusted barbed wire hedges of the Western Front? Though he had managed to stretch his positive attitude throughout the morning, this was too much. Surely Henry Ford's acclaimed masterpiece should be more reliable than this.

"Less than an hour," Grant muttered as he snapped his watch closed.

The gray-haired man who had volunteered to be Grant's driver nodded solemnly. "That's correct, sir." Robert opened the hood and peered at the motor. "Unfortunately, sir, this appears to be more serious than the last mishap."

Grant let out a sigh. He wasn't sure what annoyed him most, Robert's insistence on calling him 'sir,' the frequency with which they managed to get lost or the Model T's refusal to run more than 10 miles without a repair.

"If I translate your comment correctly, I suspect that I will have time to write my next column while you attempt to repair Mr. Ford's creation."

"Yes, sir."

Resigning himself to a long wait, Grant pulled out his traveling desk. At least the weather was pleasant, the sun shining for the first time in a week. Perhaps he would comment on that in his column. The last one had dealt with the quiet heroics of the men who spent their days in the trenches, seeing sunlight only through the narrow slit at the top of their earth-bound homes. He owed his readers a lighter subject this time.

As he opened the camp chair and settled onto it, Grant deliberately positioned himself so that he did not have to look at the reason for his delay. He should have borrowed a horse. Even though Robert had insisted that the automobile would be faster than one of the half-starved nags that were all that civilians could expect, Grant no longer believed that. Horses were reliable. They didn't lose wheels or throw bolts or do whatever it was that had caused the latest problem.

Grant turned and contemplated the object of his disgust. The only good thing he could say about the Model T was that when it died, which event appeared to be imminent, he would feel no sorrow, whereas if a horse died, he would . . . Grant shook his head. He wouldn't think about animals dying and their effect on him. He wouldn't think about the people who . . . No! That pain was part of the distant past. He was no longer a vulnerable child. He was a grown man who knew better than to let himself be hurt. Grant picked up his pen. He would write, as he had so often over the years, for one of the lessons he had learned was that writing was the way to exorcise demons.

Tanks, the experts in the War Department inform us, will transform warfare, rendering modern maneuvers obsolete. These mechanical marvels, we are told, suffer from none of the shortcomings of the common horse. They need no farriers; they do not succumb to disease; they are unaffected by the elements. While this writer does not have the audacity to contradict the collective wisdom of our military experts, he feels compelled to point out the similarities between these highly touted tanks and Mr. Ford's Model T, whose mechanical reliability has been the subject of several books.

Grant couldn't help smiling as he penned the final words. Although the automobile was indeed one of the marvels of the 20th century, its propensity for breakdowns had spawned not one but several volumes of jokes.

When this war was over—Grant would not believe the French and English soldiers who were convinced it would never end—he would pay a visit to Henry Ford. He wanted to meet the man who had had such a profound effect on American society. But that was in the future. Today all he wanted was to reach Calais. There, if luck was with him, he would be able to exchange Robert's Model T for a horse. And, if he was very, very lucky, he would find a story.

Chapter Two

The grizzled man stared at the object of Grant's disgust for a long moment, then tipped his head to one side, as if choosing his words carefully. It wasn't, Grant knew, that Monsieur Renard was seeking the correct English phrase, because they had been speaking French. Grant's own fluency in the language, eliminating the need for an interpreter, was one of the assets he had brought to his job. He wasn't sure whether it was the fact that there was no third person listening to their conversations or whether it was his occasionally halting speech that had helped him gain people's confidence. All he knew was that the lack of an interpreter had proven to be a boon and that by speaking French he had learned things that had been hidden from other, more seasoned correspondents who knew only English.

Grant had been thankful for the advantage as he had interviewed soldiers and civilians throughout France. His linguistic skill had also been helpful when he'd needed to ask directions, buy food or find lodging. For some unknown reason Monsieur Renard was not responding as the majority of his countrymen did. While Grant had dealt with the normal French reserve, this man seemed taciturn rather than reserved.

"Excuse me, monsieur," Grant said, repeating his question, "but I wondered if you might be aware of a horse that I could hire or perhaps even buy."

When they had reached Calais, Grant had insisted that Robert take them to the best livery stable. His lips twitching in what Grant assumed was an attempt not to smile, Robert had driven to a building adorned with a painting of a handsome horse. That was the only sign of four-legged transportation that Grant had seen.

"A horse, monsieur," he repeated.

Monsieur Renard shrugged in what Grant considered to be the quintessential Gallic gesture. "If anyone in Calais can fix that Tin Lizzie, it's Emily Wentworth."

The day, though overcast, was bright. There was no reason Grant should have felt as if a cloud were obscuring every ray of sunlight, plunging him into darkness, simply because the Frenchman's response was not the one he sought. Grant clenched his jaw and tried to keep his voice even. He didn't want that blasted automobile repaired. He wanted dependable transportation. "I would prefer a horse," he said firmly.

This time Monsieur Renard shook his head. "*Malheureusement.*" It didn't matter whether the word was pronounced in French or English. Grant hated it either way. *Unfortunately, malheureusement.* When a sentence began that way, Grant knew that he would not like the way it ended. "Unfortunately," the man said, repeating the hated word, "a horse is one thing I do not have." He gestured toward the empty stable. "If monsieur would like a mule . . ." The Frenchman let his words trail off.

Grant shook his head. Mules' notoriously unpleasant dispositions made even the breakdown-prone automobile Robert had provided seem like an attractive form of transportation. Speaking of Robert, where was the man? He'd disappeared as soon as he had introduced Grant to Monsieur Renard.

"All right," Grant said, resignation coloring his voice. "Let's find this wonder-working Miss Wentworth." She would be an American, Grant guessed, for in his experience few English women knew how to repair an automobile. And, judging from the gleam that suddenly lit the Frenchman's eyes, Miss Wentworth was an attractive American. For the first time since he and Robert had limped into Calais in their less than reliable Tin Lizzie, Grant felt a spark of optimism. He had been looking for a cheerful subject for his column. Perhaps Miss Wentworth and her unusual talents were what he sought.

As Grant and the former hostler approached the car, Robert emerged from the adjoining building, a new pipe clenched between his teeth. He had lost his pipe two days earlier and had complained bitterly to Grant. At first Grant had been skeptical, for it had been over a week since Robert had had tobacco, but the man had insisted that simply clenching the pipe helped soothe his nerves. While Robert had said nothing more, Grant assumed that it had been his own frustration with the Model T that had caused Robert's nerves to be in need of soothing. If a little grousing had that effect, perhaps Grant needed more than a new motor car. Perhaps he needed a different driver.

"She works for the hospital," Monsieur Renard explained as Robert drove them toward the outskirts of Calais, "but if the ambulances are running fine, she'll help others." There was no need to ask who 'she' was. In the Frenchman's eyes, there was only one woman in Calais worthy of discussion, and that was the highly esteemed and presumably attractive Emily Wentworth.

As Robert turned the car onto a narrow lane, Grant studied the building they were approaching. Judging from the symmetrical lines and the gables with bull's eye windows, he guessed that the chateau-turned-hospital dated from the 16th century. It was both a beautiful building and one that had been built to withstand attacks. That was, Grant knew, why it was perched on top of a small hill—to provide the maximum warning of approaching enemies. Unfortunately, the tactics of war had changed in the last 400 years. Now the enemy didn't always march toward a target. Grant could only hope that the huge red cross that decorated the roof would protect the building and its inhabitants from aerial attacks.

Robert parked the car, and the three men climbed out.

"Emily, I've brought you a new customer." As they approached the open door of what had obviously once been a stable, there was no ignoring the way the Frenchman's gait increased or the way he straightened his shoulders. Grant revised his estimate of the woman he was about to meet. Judging from his companion's behavior, Miss Wentworth wasn't simply attractive; she was *very* attractive.

"*Bonjour*, Monsieur Renard." The voice that emanated from the stable was lower than Grant had expected, a rich alto filled with apparent pleasure at either the Frenchman's arrival or the fact that he had brought a customer. Seconds later, the owner of the voice emerged, blinking rapidly as her eyes tried to adjust to the sunlight. Grant could feel his own eyes widen in surprise. No wonder Monsieur Renard had been so anxious for an excuse to visit. Miss Emily Wentworth wasn't simply very attractive. She was breathtakingly beautiful.

Oh, she wasn't beautiful in the way that some of the Hollywood film stars were. This woman wasn't petite with generously rounded curves. Instead, she was taller than the average American woman. Grant guessed she was a full five feet eight inches high, placing her at least three inches taller than most of her countrywomen. Instead of the curves that many men seemed to prefer, Miss Wentworth had what he would term an athletic build. The curves were there, but they were subtle. This woman was svelte, her beauty all the more striking for the fact that it was understated. She had rolled up her sleeves, revealing beautifully formed forearms, and though high button boots hid her ankles from his gaze, the graceful way she moved told Grant that her nether limbs were as well formed as her arms.

Then there was her face. It was a perfect oval, framed by ash blond hair. While other women had bobbed their hair, Emily Wentworth had left hers long. Right now it was pulled back in one of those knots that women called chignons, although a few strands had come loose and were teasing the curve of her chin. Her eyes, he noted, were light blue, more the color of an April sky than one in August. Those blue eyes regarded him steadily, as if being subject to a man's curiosity was such a commonplace event that it had no power to disconcert her. A woman like that, Grant imagined, must have spent her whole life being the object of stares.

She nodded, as if acknowledging his stare, and as she did, she began to smile. Grant watched, bemused, as dimples formed at the corners of her mouth. That was one thing he would not have expected. The rest of her was so smooth, a study in flowing lines, that he would not have imagined something as mundane as dimples.

To Grant's chagrin, Monsieur Renard began to chuckle. "Miss Wentworth, I'd like to present this gentleman to you. Unfortunately . . ." There it was again, that word Grant disliked. "Unfortunately, I do not know his name."

"Grant Randall."

Although the woman's eyes widened slightly, it was the Frenchman who reacted. "A pox on Robert," he declared. "He should have told me who you were."

Feeling almost Gallic, Grant shrugged. "I asked him not

to." One thing he had learned during his 12 months in France was that people frequently responded with more candor if unaware that they were speaking to a writer. "But," he said with a wry smile, "now that you know my name, can you find me a horse?"

"*Malheureusement*, no."

"I was afraid of that."

Emily Wentworth came a step closer. She wore a dark blue skirt with buttons down one side and a white shirtwaist that now bore a smudge on one sleeve. "Why would you want a horse when you have a Model T?" Though her voice was low and even, Grant heard genuine puzzlement in it. "This isn't just a Model T. It's an early 1911." She acted as if that was something special.

"I don't care how old it is. A horse is more reliable," Grant said. He frowned at the tall black vehicle that Robert had somehow coaxed into running once more. It was a minor miracle that it had managed to climb the hill to the hospital. "This conveyance breaks down so often that it and not the geyser in Yellowstone should be called Old Faithful."

Emily Wentworth smiled, and those surprisingly endearing dimples reappeared. "Leave it here. I'll see what I can do."

She looked behind Grant and nodded. Surprised, he turned and saw that half a dozen men were approaching. For the first time since they'd arrived at Emily Wentworth's workshop, Robert spoke. "The staff at the hospital would like to meet you."

Grant flashed the men a quick smile as he shook his head. "Later," he promised. "I want to see what Miss Wentworth discovers."

Monsieur Renard grinned and said something in rapid idiomatic French that sounded like, "The scenery is better out here." Grant could not argue with that. It wasn't, of course, the reason he was staying near the stable.

The tall blonde appeared not to have heard the French-man's comment, or perhaps she had not understood him. "You're like a medieval knight," she told Grant, "reluctant to be parted from your steed."

The image was so ludicrous that it was all Grant could do not to laugh. "To the contrary, I cherish the hope that you'll discover it has a terminal disease and will put it—and me—out of misery."

"That's unlikely," she said as she opened the hood and looked inside. "It probably needs a new part." She placed a wrench on something within the motor and tightened it slightly.

"Will I make you nervous if I watch?"

As soon as Emily opened the hood, Robert and Monsieur Renard had disappeared with the other men, presumably to sample some of the hospital chef's pastries. As they'd driven from Monsieur Renard's stable to the hospital, the Frenchman had told Grant that the chef's culinary skills were legendary, almost as famous as Miss Wentworth's ability to repair automobiles.

Emily turned to look at Grant, her blue eyes sparkling with mirth. "Isn't that what you intended—to make me so nervous that I'd make a mistake and then the car wouldn't run at all?"

"Do you think I'm capable of such despicable motives?" She wasn't far off the mark, though Grant had no intention of admitting that. Nor would he admit that her smile was brightening a less than perfect day, or that it had been a long time since he'd had a conversation with a young and beautiful woman.

That young and beautiful woman arched an eyebrow. "Mr. Randall, I suspect you're a man who will let nothing stand between him and his goals."

"You're very astute, Miss Wentworth. I am a man who believes in achieving goals." And today's goal was finding reliable transportation. "But please call me Grant. 'Mr. Randall' makes me feel a hundred years old."

"I'll do that, if you call me Emily."

"Agreed, Emily. Now, let's see what you're going to do to Black Beauty."

"The car is blue, you know."

Grant pushed his spectacles back on his nose and stared at the vehicle. Though his eyesight was far from perfect, he was not colorblind. "It looks like black to me."

"The newer models are black," she admitted, "but the 1911s were almost all painted this very dark blue." When Grant shrugged, Emily continued, "A lot of people think it's black. I just assumed that since you're so precise in your descriptions, you'd want to know the facts."

She moved with quiet assurance, tapping a part, tightening another, peering intently at a third. Unlike Robert, whose attempts to repair the automobile had been at best fumbling, Emily appeared to know exactly what to do. Grant took a step closer, watching as she bent over the motor, her slender hands with their long fingers moving gracefully from one part of the engine to another.

Grant had met hundreds, perhaps thousands, of women in his life, but none had had Emily Wentworth's combination of beauty, wit and . . . he searched for the word. Spunk. That was it. She was spunky. And he was a fool for noticing. Hadn't he learned his lessons years ago? What mattered today was getting reliable transportation. Emily Wentworth was nothing more than the means to that goal. If Grant had any sense at all, he would leave her to work and would join the men inside. The spring breeze might be soft and the day warm enough to make a man enjoy being outdoors, but it was wiser—safer—to leave. Grant was an expert at leaving.

He turned and took a step toward the hospital.

"That's it!"

Grant stopped in mid-stride. "You found something." Her triumphant cry made him phrase his response as a statement, not a question.

Emily looked up, her face wreathed with a smile. "It's a cracked spark plug wire." She pointed toward the offending part. "I wonder how it ran at all."

Grant couldn't help chuckling. "I wouldn't call the last day's travel running. We spent as much time by the side of the road as we did moving." He stared at the wire that Emily had unfastened and which clearly had a crack in it. "I wonder how Robert fixed it. He never said anything about a spark plug wire." Privately, Grant suspected that Robert had no idea there were wires of any sort in the motor.

Emily pulled a wire from her toolbox and began to attach it. "Robert probably jostled it when he was working on something else. That could have been enough to let the current flow until vibrations broke the connection again." And, Grant remembered, the rutted road had provided its share of vibrations.

"So now it's fixed?"

Emily nodded. "Indeed, it is. Do you want to give it a test drive?"

Grant shook his head. "My only attempts at driving were disastrous."

If Emily was surprised by his admission, she said nothing. She looked at the sky, as if assessing whether rain was imminent. When Monsieur Renard had joined them, Robert had folded the top down.

"I don't want to send the car out without a test." Emily reached for her hat and tied it firmly beneath her chin. She had apparently decided to keep the top down. "Do you want to come with me?"

He ought to refuse. He could use the excuse of having

to meet the hospital staff. That was valid. He did not have to tell Emily that he was reluctant to spend more time with her, that the odd sense of connection he had felt when he had first seen her had alarmed him. It would disappear, of course. He would make sure of that. After all, he would leave Calais tomorrow, and Emily Wentworth would become only a distant memory.

He ought to refuse. He would refuse. He did not.

"How long have you been in France?" he asked 10 minutes later, when they had reached the edge of Calais. Though Grant did not consider himself an expert on the internal combustion engine, even his untrained ear could hear the difference between the sound the automobile was now making and the sputtering that had been so common on the drive into the city. Emily Wentworth was indeed a miracle worker where Henry Ford's inventions were concerned. She was also a skilled driver, navigating smoothly around the largest ruts in the road, seeming to turn the vehicle effortlessly.

"I've been here a month," she said. "Why did you ask?"

"You obviously know these roads well. You must have taken them often." They had passed quickly through Calais and were now on the other side.

Emily shook her head, and another strand of hair dislodged itself from her chignon. "It's the first time I've been this way. All the driving I've done has been from the hospital to the train station."

Grant couldn't mask his surprise. "Then how do you keep from getting lost? Or are we lost?" He doubted it, for she had taken branches in the road with such assurance that he felt confident she knew exactly where she was headed. While this road looked to Grant to be identical to every other one in this part of France—its edges lined with poplars, the farmhouses gray stone with darker gray slate roofs—Emily appeared able to distinguish it from the others.

"We're not lost," she said, confirming his assumption. "I've studied every map of France I could find. I thought it would be important that I could drive the ambulance anywhere it might have to go."

Grant had spent years observing people, hearing what was left unsaid as well as what they revealed. That experience told him that while Emily was not lying, she also wasn't telling him the whole story. He didn't doubt that she had studied maps. The evidence was clear that she had. But, if he were a betting man, Grant would have wagered a substantial sum that she had reasons beyond wanting to drive an ambulance. He also knew better than to challenge her. There was more than one way to learn the truth.

"How about you?" she asked. "When did you come to France?"

Emily pushed the hand lever forward, and the car began to accelerate. Not once when Robert had driven had they achieved this speed. Emily Wentworth was indeed the miracle worker Monsieur Renard had claimed.

Grant twisted slightly in the seat and looked at the woman who had wrought such a change in the Tin Lizzie. "I came about a year ago," he said. "I volunteered as soon as President Wilson declared war, because I wanted to do something." Grant waited for her to ask the obvious question, why he wasn't serving on the front lines with so many other Americans. But Emily Wentworth did not ask. Like Grant himself, she appeared willing to wait for confidences. And so he told her, tapping his spectacles. "Even with these, my eyesight isn't good enough for me to be drafted. The Army was afraid I'd hit one of our men instead of the enemy."

It was only a slight exaggeration. His poor eyesight had shaped Grant's life in ways he preferred not to remember, with being rejected by the Army only the latest in a long string of rejections. No one, it seemed, wanted a boy—or a man—who was less than perfect.

Emily turned slightly, and to Grant's surprise he saw neither pity nor disgust on her face. Instead he saw an emotion that was far less common than either of them. "So you found another way to help."

The admiration in Emily's voice warmed Grant more than the summer sun. He shouldn't let himself care what she thought. It was foolish. But, Grant told himself, little harm could come of enjoying this afternoon. Tomorrow it would be nothing more than a memory.

"Have you wanted to be a writer for a long time?" Emily asked.

That was a question he could answer. "For as long as I can remember. I once thought I would write fiction." It was safe to tell her that, though he had no intention of divulging the reason. No one needed to know that Grant had learned the value of imaginary friends at an early age. Unlike real ones, they didn't die or desert him.

He looked down the road, wondering where Emily was headed. From the way she drove, he guessed she had a specific destination in mind. He wouldn't ask, though. Instead, he would learn what he could about this extraordinary woman. "I know you haven't been an ambulance driver for as long as I've been a writer." She appeared to be little older than 20, a veritable youngster compared to his own 28 years. "What brought you to France?"

Emily shrugged as if the answer were inconsequential, but Grant noted that she did not meet his gaze. Instead, she stared intently at the windscreen, as if she found this stretch of road fascinating. When she spoke, her voice was calm. "The same thing that brings most people. I wanted to do my share."

She was lying.

* * *

She hated lying to him. She had almost grown accustomed to the evasions and half truths that had become a part of her life, to the point where she felt only a twinge of discomfort when she prevaricated. But this was different. It was more than discomfort that Emily felt when she lied to Grant Randall; it was an ache, as real as if she had eaten too many green persimmons.

It shouldn't have happened. There was no reason she should feel this way, any more than there was a reason why she should have felt the almost electrical shock that seemed to pass between them when she had stepped out of the stable and had seen him. They hadn't even touched, and yet she had felt it, as surely as if she had shorted a wire in Gertie's motor. Emily hadn't been expecting that, any more than she had expected Grant Randall to suddenly appear in her garage. Twenty-four hours ago she hadn't even known the man's name, and now here he was, disturbing the tenuous peace that she'd made with herself.

He didn't look at all the way she had imagined. When Sarah had read the columns to her, Emily had pictured an older man—50 at least—with stooped shoulders, graying hair and a face well-lined by time. Surely a man as young as Grant Randall, who couldn't be over 30, hadn't experienced enough of life to display the sensitivity that was the hallmark of his writing. His shoulders weren't stooped. Far from it. Instead, though he stood at least half a foot taller than Emily, making him more than six feet tall, he walked with almost military precision, his head and shoulders held erect. His hair was dark brown, almost as dark as his eyes, and only his nose kept his face from being perfect. Oddly, the crooked nose seemed to add to his appeal, making him seem more human.

"What happened to your nose?" The instant the words were out of her mouth, Emily felt her face flush. How could she have said anything so rude? But Grant did not appear to find her question prying.

"It got broken in a fight when I was seven."

Emily rubbed her forearm, then laid her hand back on the steering wheel. This car was older than the ambulances and needed a firmer grip to keep it moving in a straight line. "That must have hurt," she said, grimacing at the remembered pain. "I broke my arm at the same age, and it still hurts sometimes."

"When it rains." Grant's words were a statement, not a question, although he followed with one. "How did you break your arm? I doubt you were in a fight."

He would laugh when he heard the tale. For a second, Emily considered inventing a more conventional story. Then she shrugged. Grant Randall looked like a man who rarely laughed. Everyone needed to laugh. Even if he was laughing at her expense, what mattered was the laughter itself.

"I fell out of a tree."

He didn't laugh. Instead, Grant gave her an appraising look that seemed to be tinged with admiration. "You're a surprising woman, Emily Wentworth. None of the girls I knew climbed trees."

Emily looked at the poplars that lined the road, trying to imagine climbing one. "My sisters didn't," she admitted. "It was only Theo and I who had contests to see who could go higher in the live oaks." With their thick spreading branches, live oaks were well suited to climbing, unlike the slender upright poplars.

Though Grant had been peering through the windscreen, he turned and fixed his gaze on her. "Is Theo your brother?"

"My twin." Emily bit the inside of her mouth, trying to hold back the pain that thoughts of Theo brought. Though no one in the family had doubted the special closeness the twins shared, they had been skeptical when Emily and Theo had claimed that they always knew when one of them needed the other. The day that Emily had fallen from the tree, no one could hear her shouting, but somehow Theo knew where she was and dragged their mother there, insisting his sister was hurt.

Emily rubbed her arm again. Though the break had healed long ago, when she thought of that day, the bone throbbed, reminding her of her brother. Today the pain was more than physical, for with it came the conviction that Theo needed her, the same conviction that had brought Emily to France. But she had no intention of telling Grant Randall that. She had already revealed too much to him.

"You must have seen a lot of France," Emily said, deliberately changing the subject. "Have you been to a town called Goudot?"

Grant was silent for a moment. "I don't think so. Why?"

"My sister Carolyn's there. She's a nurse at the base hospital."

As Emily had hoped, Grant seized the new topic. "You mentioned sisters—plural—before. Where are the others?"

These were safe subjects, ones where Emily had no need to lie. "There's only one other. That's my oldest sister Martha, and she's at home."

"And where is home?" Grant squinted through his spectacles, as if he were trying to see behind Emily's words. It was a disconcerting thought.

Emily frowned. "I feel as if I'm being interviewed." Admittedly, this was better than talking about Theo, but Emily wasn't used to being the center of attention. That had always been Carolyn's role. Once the beautiful Carolyn Wentworth entered a room, no one noticed Emily. Though Carolyn was 100 miles away, Emily had grown so accustomed to fading into the background that it felt odd to be the focus of a man's attention. Particularly a handsome man.

"I assure you you're not being interviewed." Grant flashed her a self-deprecating smile. "I'm more subtle when I'm interviewing someone."

"Then why are you asking so many questions?"

The question appeared to give him pause. "Perhaps it's because I've never met a woman who could fix a Model T," he said at last.

"Ah, yes, my sole claim to fame." And, if Sarah's supposition was correct, that was more a liability than an asset.

"It's a very valuable skill," Grant said. "But you still haven't told me where home is."

Emily shrugged. "A town in Texas called Canela. It's much smaller than Calais."

Though Grant seemed unaware, the route Emily was taking was a large circle, designed to avoid having to drive the same road twice. They had reached one of the higher points in the city, a vantage from which they could see the English Channel. Emily pressed the clutch pedal to slow the car.

"Do you know what that is?" Grant asked, pointing toward a medieval-looking stone tower.

Emily nodded. It was one of the reasons she had come this way. "It's about the only landmark I recognize. I've been told it's called the Tour du Guet—Guet Tower in English—and that it used to be a lighthouse."

"Twelfth or thirteenth century, I'd guess."

Emily turned to stare at Grant. "You'd be right. It's from the thirteenth century. Now it's my turn to ask a question. How did you know that? Did you study medieval architecture?"

Grant shook his head. "Nothing so formal. Being a correspondent means I talk to a lot of people. I discovered that they like to talk about their homes, when they were built, things like that. They'd relax when they did that, and as a bonus, I learned to recognize different periods." He pushed his glasses back onto his nose. "Most buildings are big enough that I can see them."

Emily suspected that Grant's vision was not as bad as he claimed but that he used it to disarm people, to make them forget that he was Grant Randall, the famous war correspondent. It was, she guessed, a good tactic.

"Do you know what time it is?" she asked, suddenly aware that they had been gone for longer than the quarter hour she had originally expected.

He pulled out his watch. "Four-thirty."

Later than she had hoped. "I need to get back to the hospital," she said as she put the car into gear. "It's almost time for the train." Twice a day trains of wounded arrived, and twice a day Emily drove the ambulance that brought men from the station to the hospital.

They were halfway back when she heard the cries. At first she thought she had imagined it, but when she heard the sound again, Emily put her foot on the brake and pulled the hand lever into neutral. "Oh, Grant, look!" She jumped from the car and made her way through the thick grass. There, huddled at the base of a tree, was a tiny orange kitten. The long gashes in its fur and the blood that caked its face left no doubt about the reason the kitten was crying. "The poor thing's been hurt." Knowing that the animal might scratch and claw, Emily returned to Grant's car and opened the toolbox. She had brought it in case the Model T needed additional repairs, never thinking that the towel she kept to wipe her hands would serve as a blanket for an injured kitten.

"It's going to be all right," Emily crooned to the tiny animal as she wrapped it and carried it to the car. "We're taking you to a hospital," she said. "They'll know what to do with you."

Surely it was Emily's imagination that Grant looked as if he pitied her when she handed him the kitten. It was the kitten who deserved pity, not Emily. But Grant, it appeared, had no sympathy to spare for a wounded animal. Though he allowed the cat to remain on his lap where Emily had placed it, not once during the drive back to the hospital did he glance at it. The easy camaraderie that they had shared had disappeared. Instead of the light banter and gentle questions that had marked their time together, now there was silence, punctuated only by the kitten's anguished cries.

Emily drove as fast as she dared, concentrating on the road in front of her rather than the man who sat at her side, as silent and motionless as a statue. What was wrong with him, Emily wanted to know as she rounded the last corner. Was he made of steel rather than flesh and blood like normal humans? Was that why he could sit there, apparently unmoved by the kitten's mewing?

It was all Emily could do to hold back her tears. But crying would solve nothing. She knew that. What the kitten needed was medical care, not crying. It was Emily's job to get the poor creature to the hospital and convince one of the doctors to treat it.

As for Grant? Emily darted a glance at the man whose writing evoked such a range of emotions. Perhaps he was made of steel; perhaps he had to be. Perhaps that was the only way he could cope with the horrors he had seen and still be able to infuse optimism into his writing. He had built a protective shell around his emotions; that had to be the reason he could sit there, unfazed by the cat's suffering. The alternative—that Grant Randall had been born without feelings—was unthinkable.

Chapter Three

"**H**e's doing what?" Emily looked up from her clipboard. Though it was only a few miles to the train station, she took no chances and had developed a list of things to check before she pulled the ambulance out of the stable.

Sarah's grin told Emily that she was enjoying being the bearer of these particular tidings. "Grant Randall is coming with us. I heard him tell Dr. Mercer that he hadn't ever observed doctors working in an ambulance, and he thought it was time to—as he said—remedy that deficiency. I think he's planning to write a column about the doctors."

That was, Emily knew, what the doctors wished would happen. She had heard them speculating on the reason for Grant's visit to the hospital and how they hoped he would spend an extra day or two with them, seeing the difference between this hospital and the field units he had described in earlier columns.

Sarah straightened her shoulders and pushed a pair of imaginary spectacles back onto her nose. "We'll see, gentlemen."

Emily couldn't help smiling at the way her friend had captured Grant Randall's midwestern inflection. The

31

woman was a natural mimic. Sarah was also a first rate nurse. "What about you?" Emily asked as she hoisted a can of gasoline onto the running board. Though it was unlikely she would need it for the short trips to and from the hospital, protocol required every ambulance to carry extra fuel and oil along with a spare tire.

Emily turned back to Sarah. "I'm not arguing that doctors aren't vital, but nurses' roles are just as important. Grant Randall ought to write about you."

To Emily's surprise, Sarah flushed. "You're saying that because your sister is a nurse."

"I'm saying it because it's true," Emily countered. She picked up her clipboard and resumed her checking. Because of her drive with Grant and the time she had spent with the kitten, Emily was behind schedule. She would have to hurry now to ensure that the ambulances would arrive at the station before the train.

"I watch all of you at work," she told Sarah. "It's obvious that you're a team, and everyone on that team is important. You can't win a baseball game if you only have hitters; you need pitchers and catchers too."

Sarah handed Emily the large box of medical supplies that was always placed on the passenger's side running board. "If you say so. You know a lot more about sports than I do." Sarah shrugged and picked up her cape. "I think what we nurses do is important, but I doubt Grant Randall will notice. He hasn't featured a woman in his column for as long as I've been reading it."

Sarah turned her cape so that the coveted red lining was obvious. Though Sarah had never said anything, Emily knew that only Red Cross nurses had red linings in their capes and were permitted to wear the red cross insignia on their sleeves. Other nurses' uniforms were similar but lacked those two distinguishing features.

"I wonder if he dislikes women," Sarah continued, her voice contemplative.

Emily remembered the way Grant had looked at her, the frankly appraising—and appreciative—glances he had given her. "I don't think that's the case," she said. "If anything, I'd say he doesn't want to get close to people in general—men or women."

Sarah's eyes widened in surprise. "I can't believe that." She shook her head so violently that her cap slid slightly to the left. "The way he writes about people is so beautiful."

"I don't deny that. Grant Randall crafts words that touch readers' hearts. What I question is whether his own heart is touched."

When Sarah frowned, Emily realized she might be overreacting, magnifying Grant's reaction to the kitten. When they had arrived at the hospital, it had looked almost as if he were gritting his teeth as he handed the wounded animal to her. The doctors, who had grown accustomed to Emily's habit of rescuing stray animals, had simply nodded and cleared a space on an operating table. The kitten, they told her half an hour later, had needed nothing more than a few stitches.

"Now your garage will be mouse-free," they predicted, reminding Emily that she had complained about the presence of rodents in the former stable.

"This is my lucky day," she said, her heart lighter than it had been in weeks. She didn't care whether the kitten turned into a mouser. What mattered was that the animal's wounds would heal.

It wasn't only the rescued kitten that made Emily smile. As Dr. Mercer and Grant approached the first ambulance, she felt the same sense of excitement that she had experienced the first time she had seen Grant Randall. There was something about him that drew her to him, almost the way a magnet drew iron filings. The analogy was a good one, Emily realized, for she didn't want to be attracted. She had a mission to accomplish, and nothing could be allowed to interfere with that mission. But, like the filings and the magnet, the force was too great to ignore.

"Emily, have you met Grant Randall?" Dr. Mercer smiled at Emily, then gestured toward the man at his side. With his dark hair and eyes, Grant Randall might have been mistaken for a Frenchman, were it not for his height. Though the hospital staff considered Dr. Mercer a big man, Grant stood several inches taller, making him literally a head taller than most Frenchmen.

"Indeed she has," Grant said. "This is the woman who saved my Model T from the scrap heap."

As the doctor began to applaud, Emily shrugged. "I'm afraid Mr. Randall is exaggerating. The real story is that I replaced a broken wire."

"That's our Emily." Dr. Mercer's grin was warm and friendly. "She doesn't realize how valuable she is." He turned to his guest. "Grant, why don't you sit in front with her? The view is better there."

He directed Grant toward Gertie, the ambulance Emily would be driving today. She and Gaston, the other driver, alternated between Gertie, which was equipped for ambulatory patients, accommodating four men in its rear compartment, and the second ambulance, which the staff had named Lucille. With space for two stretchers, Lucille was reserved for the more seriously wounded patients.

Grant gave Emily an appraising glance. "Indeed, the view is better there."

To Emily's chagrin, she felt heat rise in her cheeks. "The important things happen in the back," she said.

"And he'll join us there for the return trip," the doctor agreed. "Come on, Emily. Show him how well you drive."

He sat beside her as he had earlier that afternoon. His

long legs were stretched out in front of him as they had been before. That much was the same. But much was different. She didn't look the same, and she didn't feel the same. Emily had changed from her work clothes into one of the gray cotton uniforms that were issued to nurses and which the hospital had suggested she wear when she drive, since it marked her as part of the staff. That was one difference.

The vehicle wasn't the same. Instead of Grant's Model T touring car, they were now in the ambulance. Although the front compartment was similar to Grant's motor car with its open sides and leather seat, the canvas roof was permanently attached, and the longer body made it more difficult to maneuver. That was another difference.

Most importantly, this time their mission was more serious than simply proving that Emily's repairs had cured the Tin Lizzie's problems. This time they were meeting a train of critically wounded men.

As they rounded the first corner, Grant turned toward Emily. His words were so soft that she doubted Sarah and the doctor could hear them. "I was glad to hear about the kitten," Grant said. "I know how worried you were." For a second, her eyes met his, and she could have sworn that the happiness she felt in her heart was reflected in his eyes. Then the shutters closed, and he was once again Grant Randall, the man who showed no emotion.

"I'm very relieved," she agreed, then turned her attention to navigating the vehicle around the potholes that months of rain had left in the road.

When she swerved to avoid a particularly large crater, Dr. Mercer spoke. "Nicely done," he said. Though a wall separated the two compartments, windows allowed communication between the driver and the patients in back. To Emily's surprise, the doctor extended his hand through the window and laid it on her shoulder in what she guessed was a gesture of approval. Emily tried not to recoil. Why was the doctor paying special attention to her? He'd never done it before. Wasn't it only yesterday that he'd been flirting with Sarah?

"I'd have hit that for sure," the doctor said. Emily moved ever so slightly, trying to dislodge his hand without seeming rude. As if he understood, he withdrew his hand. "I wish all our drivers were as good as you. I don't suppose you have any more like you at home."

Emily shook her head as she adjusted the spark lever. "I'm afraid not. My sisters were always too busy with other things to learn to drive." She wouldn't have learned, had it not been for Theo.

"What things interested your sisters?" Emily wasn't sure why the doctor was asking her all these questions. She had driven him to the station at least a dozen times, and he had been silent for most of those trips.

She glanced at the man who sat next to her. He was watching her; she knew that. What she didn't know was what he was thinking and whether he found Dr. Mercer's questions as unusual as she did.

"Martha teaches school," Emily said, referring to her oldest sister. "She's the smart one in the family. Carolyn's the beautiful one." Emily smiled. No one could help smiling at the middle Wentworth daughter. "She used to arrange parties at the country club, but now she's a nurse here in France."

"And what is your role?" It was Grant who asked the question.

The answer was easy. "I'm Theo's twin."

"I see." His voice was even, his expression inscrutable, giving Emily no hint of what it was he saw.

"How about you, Grant?" she asked, trying to deflect the attention from herself. "Do you have any siblings?"

"A good question, Emily." Dr. Mercer's hand was once

more on her shoulder. As Grant fixed his gaze on the doctor's hand, he removed it but continued speaking. "Grant has told us a lot about others, but his columns don't reveal anything about himself."

"That's because there's not much to tell," Grant said, his voice as calm as if he were reporting the weather. "I grew up near Chicago, and I have no siblings. End of story."

But it wasn't. Emily knew that. Though his words were probably true, she was certain he had not revealed the whole truth, just as she was certain she would not pry. It was obvious that Grant did not want people learning more about his life, and—since she did not want too close a scrutiny of her own stories—she would respect that. But she couldn't help wondering what it was that Grant was hiding and why he felt it necessary to resort to half truths.

With a wry smile, Emily reflected that it was ironic that she had become an expert on more than repairing automobiles. Now she was an expert in recognizing half truths. That was truly unfortunate.

Grant stood at the side of the depot, watching as men were transferred from the hospital train to the ambulance. Though he had brought no paper and pen with him, he was taking mental notes. The scene was not what he had expected. For one thing, it was less chaotic than the admittance of the wounded to field hospitals. That was, Grant suspected, the result of the fact that these patients had been stabilized. When men were brought to the field hospitals, many of them had had only the most rudimentary of first aid. By the time they reached a base hospital like the one in Calais, they had received some treatment. And, though Grant didn't want to admit it, the most seriously wounded never made it past the field hospitals.

Here, though there was an undeniable sense of urgency, there was also an orderliness to the way the men were handled. It was almost as if someone had choreographed the steps each member of the medical team would take. The orderlies removed the men from the train cars; the nurses consulted their records and pointed the doctors toward the most critically wounded. Everyone had a role, including Emily. And that surprised Grant.

He had thought that her role was simply to drive the ambulance. Surely that was enough. Surely that was all a driver was supposed to do. But Emily did more. Rather than remain in the vehicle, she helped the orderlies carry the stretchers. Most women would not have done that. Most women would not have had the strength to lift a stretcher. But Emily Wentworth was not most women.

She didn't stop with simple transportation. Instead, Grant noticed that she spoke to each one of the men. He didn't hear what she said, but whatever she murmured seemed to reassure them. Or perhaps it was her beautiful face that eased the pain. Grant knew that if he were wounded—or even if he weren't—he would prefer to look at Emily rather than the doctor or even Nurse Gilmore.

It was obvious the doctor felt the same way. He couldn't have made his intentions more clear if he'd telegraphed them. All those smiles, followed by the questions. And then there were the touches. Grant clenched his teeth. It wasn't his business if Dr. Mercer was courting Emily Wentworth. He shouldn't care. He *didn't* care. Romance wasn't a part of Grant Randall's life. It never had been. It never would be.

Grant wasn't sure which Roman had claimed that a rolling stone gathered no moss, but when he'd heard the maxim, he had adopted it as his motto. He would keep moving, gathering nothing that would weigh him down, nothing that could cause him pain. He would leave Calais soon, perhaps even tomorrow. And then Emily Wentworth would be nothing more than a faint memory. That was how it had always been and how it needed to be.

Grant climbed into the back of the ambulance and watched as Dr. Mercer and Nurse Gilmore treated the patients. They were good. There was no denying that. They worked with quiet precision, checking vital signs on the most seriously wounded men but always seeming to be aware of all the patients under their care.

And in the front of the vehicle was the most unusual woman Grant had ever met. It wasn't simply that Emily did things other women did not. What made her unusual was that she seemed unaware of her own value. Though he doubted Emily had realized it, her descriptions of her sisters had revealed a great deal about Emily herself. It was apparent that she had grown up in the shadow of her older sisters and that they had somehow been allowed to eclipse Emily, so much so that she didn't recognize her unique talents. What a shame!

She was beautiful and smart and doing her share—perhaps more than her share—in this horrible war. Someone ought to tell her that. Someone ought to show Emily just how special she was, just as someone ought to tell her not to care so much about wounded animals. Someone ought to warn her that by caring too much she was opening herself to heartbreak. Someone ought to help her, but that someone most definitely was not Grant Randall. No, sirree.

He had learned his lessons the hard way a long time ago, and he wasn't going to forget them. Absolutely not. He would leave Calais tomorrow morning. It didn't matter where he went. All that mattered was putting miles between him and Calais, between him and Emily. The more miles, the better. Soon she would be nothing more than a distant memory.

* * *

"Did you read Grant Randall's column this morning?" Sarah looked across the breakfast table at Emily. They were seated at one end of the long table that was normally reserved for the nurses. There was nothing unusual about that, just as there was nothing unusual about the low murmur of voices that filled the room or the delicious aromas of scrambled eggs and warm bread. The dining room with its centuries-old slate floor and graceful long windows looked the same as it had every other day. What was different was Sarah. Today her brown eyes sparkled more than normal, as if she were the keeper of a particularly pleasant secret.

"No, I didn't read it." Emily began to butter her toast, ensuring that each square inch of grilled bread was carefully covered. She didn't want to meet Sarah's gaze any more than she wanted to discuss Grant Randall. Emily took a bite of the toast. Chewing gave her a reason not to speak. The truth was, she had no intention of telling Sarah that she hadn't even looked at Grant's column since the day he'd left. She wouldn't admit that she didn't want to read his words and picture him saying them. It was foolish. Emily knew that. Just as she knew that it was foolish to care that he had left without a good-bye. After all, Grant Randall didn't owe her anything. He had thanked her for repairing his Model T. That was all that common courtesy required. Emily shouldn't have been hurt by the fact that he'd disappeared without telling her he was leaving. But she was.

Sarah thrust the newspaper under Emily's nose. "Read today's," she ordered. "I think you'll find it interesting."

If there was one thing Emily knew about Sarah, it was that she was persistent. She wouldn't give up until Emily at least glanced at the column. "All right," Emily said, not caring that she sounded ungracious. She took the paper and scanned the page.

UNSUNG HEROES Grant had titled it. Though she didn't

want to be, Emily was intrigued. *I've filled many inches of print with stories of our men in the trenches, the Dough-boys and poilus*, he said, referring to the nicknames the American and French soldiers had been given. *I've told you of those men who face danger on a daily basis, and I'm confident I'll do so, many more times before this dreadful war is over, but today I turn your attention to a different group of heroes, ones whose contribution to the war effort is often overlooked. I raise my glass in a toast to the men and women who drive our ambulances.*

Emily looked at Sarah. The woman's smile reminded her of the Cheshire cat in *Alice in Wonderland*. "Gaston will be pleased," Emily said, referring to the hospital's other ambulance driver.

Sarah shook her head as she placed her coffee cup back on its saucer. "You missed the point, Emily. Grant Randall is writing about you."

The sun was streaming through the long windows. That was the reason Emily blinked. It wasn't from astonishment at the nonsense Sarah was speaking. "Of course he isn't writing about me," Emily insisted. "This is a tribute to all ambulance drivers."

Though Emily hadn't thought it possible, Sarah's smile widened. "Keep reading," she said.

There was no way out. Emily continued to read, and as she did, she felt her cheeks redden, for there was no doubt Grant had quoted some of the things she had said to the wounded men. While he might be writing about all drivers, he had used her as the model for at least part of the column.

Though her manner is self-effacing, he concluded, *almost as if she were unaware of the way her quiet words and genuinely compassionate smile lighten the hearts and ease the pain of our seriously wounded men, there is no doubt this woman is one of the medical community's true treas-ures, as valuable as sutures and bandages.*

"Well?" Sarah demanded.

"He must have been writing about someone else at the end." Yes, she had said some of the things he had quoted, but she wasn't a 'true treasure.'

Sarah shook her head again. "Oh, Emily! You're hopeless."

It was silly, of course, but Emily found herself smiling at the oddest times during the day as she remembered Grant's words. They weren't about her. They couldn't be. It was simply that the man was a skilled writer, and she was admiring his talent.

That night, however, Emily did not smile, for that night she dreamed of Theo. Always in the past when she had dreamed of him, they'd been together in Texas. This dream was different. This time she was alone in France, driving an ambulance along a road that she had never before seen, and the sun was beginning to set. Somehow Emily knew that it was imperative that she reach her destination before the sun set, just as she knew that the road she was traveling was not on any map. This trip was important. More than that, it was vital.

Emily wasn't certain where she was going, and yet she knew she was not lost. Each time that she reached a crossroad, she would turn instinctively, as if something—or someone—were guiding her. In her dream, she continued driving for hours and yet the sun did not seem to move. It hovered at the edge of the horizon, turning the sky bright scarlet. No matter how far she drove or how many turns she made, the sun remained in the same position, almost as if time were at a standstill, waiting for her to reach her destination.

And then she approached a fork in the road that, like all the others, seemed familiar. Yet when she reached it, Emily did not know which way to turn. Right or left; left or right. The words echoed in her mind. The decision was important.

She knew that. What she did not know was which branch to take. Her unseen guide had disappeared, leaving in its absence a growing sense of urgency. Time was running out.

Suddenly, the sun began to slip, and Emily knew that in minutes the world would be black. She had to keep driving. There was no question now of what she was doing. She was on her way to Theo. She had to find him. His life depended on her reaching him before the sun set. But which direction should she go?

In desperation, Emily climbed out of the ambulance and walked to the fork in the road, searching for a sign. And then she heard his voice. At first she could distinguish no words; all she knew was that it was Theo's voice and that he was calling to her. The sounds faded in and out, like a weak radio transmission. Emily closed her eyes and concentrated. This was important. She knew it.

"Need you . . . Emily . . . my oh . . . my oh."

And then there was only silence.

Emily wakened, her heart pounding with fear and elation. The dream had been so real that even now she could hear her brother's words. Theo was still alive! That was wonderful. What was not wonderful was the pain Emily had heard in his voice. Theo needed her desperately. Though he had not pronounced the words, Emily knew that he was wounded—seriously wounded—and she was his final hope.

Chapter Four

This morning it was difficult to find a silver lining. Emily frowned as she studied the second ambulance's motor. The transmission shaft was bent. Though she wished she could claim otherwise, that was a serious problem. If she and Gaston continued to drive Lucille in its current state, there was the possibility that the ambulance would stop completely, leaving patients stranded between the train station and the hospital. That was one thing Emily could not allow to happen. In a perfect world, she would replace the shaft. Unfortunately, this was not a perfect world.

Resolutely, Emily walked to her toolbox. She knew that there were no spare transmission shafts in Calais and probably not anywhere in France. That left her only one alternative. She would have to try to straighten the one that she had. On a good day, though that would not be an easy task, she would welcome the challenge. Today was not a good day. Fixing Lucille would demand strength, but Emily was exhausted.

She could not remember ever feeling so tired. Part of it was physical. After she had dreamed of Theo and had wakened with the knowledge that he needed her, sleep had

eluded her. Instead of getting the rest she required if she
were to think coherently, she had lain awake, trying to complete Theo's sentence.

My oh . . . what? What word started with the sound
"oh"? Old, oak, oath. None of the words that she could
remember made any sense. At four in the morning, when
she had realized that sleep would not come, Emily had paid
a visit to the hospital's small library and had consulted an
English dictionary. It was to no avail. None of the words
sparked her imagination. That was when physical exhaus-
tion combined with mental anguish. Theo needed her. The
fear that she would fail her brother drained Emily's energy
as much as the lack of sleep did.

She placed a large wrench on the transmission shaft and
began to turn it, hoping that the steady pressure would
straighten the shaft enough that the ambulance would be
safe to drive. Emily gritted her teeth as she tried to torque
the wrench. If she could repair the ambulance, at least she
would feel that something good had happened today.

She tightened her grip on the wrench and gave it another
quarter turn. The shaft was beginning to straighten. One
more turn, and it would be fixed. Perhaps that was a good
omen. Emily twisted the wrench once more, then smiled
with satisfaction. And as she did, she heard footsteps on
the stone floor. It wasn't Gaston. She knew his slightly
shuffling gait. And it wasn't Sarah. Her footsteps were
lighter.

Emily looked up. It took less than a second, but she
could feel the blood drain from her face, then rush back,
staining her cheeks as bright a red as the lining of Sarah's
cape. What was *he* doing here?

"Hello, Grant," Emily said, pleased that her voice did
not betray the confusion his arrival had created. She replaced the wrench in the toolbox, then took a step toward
the man who had, if Sarah was to be believed, described

Emily as a 'true treasure,' the same man who had left Calais without saying farewell.

Emily straightened her skirt. It was ridiculous to wish she were wearing a pretty frock rather than her serviceable navy-blue skirt and white shirtwaist. Undoubtedly Grant had returned to have his car serviced. He hadn't come to see her. Of course he hadn't.

"I didn't expect you." Emily counted it a minor miracle that her voice continued to sound perfectly normal. She knew her cheeks were still flushed, but that could be from exertion. She had, after all, just straightened a bent transmission shaft. "Is your flivver having problems again?"

Grant took another step, closing the distance between them. He was now close enough that she could smell the slightly astringent scent of soap. Emily's glance flickered over him. Though it was dry, his hair looked as if it had been washed recently.

Grant Randall was every bit as handsome as she had remembered, his brown eyes sparkling behind his glasses, his lips curved into a wry smile. "No problems," he said, and his voice sent a shiver down her spine. "Hortense has been running perfectly ever since you replaced the wire."

"You named the car." That surprised Emily almost as much as Grant's return to Calais.

He shrugged. "You named your ambulances. Besides," he added as he pushed his glasses back onto his nose, "I have this delusion that if I treat the flivver—as you call it—with respect, perhaps it will continue to run."

"Henry Ford might not refer to his creation that way, but the term 'flivver' is used by as many people as 'Tin Lizzie.' " It was ridiculous. They were standing in the doorway of the garage, discussing nicknames for the Model T, when what Emily wanted to know was why Grant had come back to Calais. If his car—Hortense, Emily corrected herself—did not need repairs, she could not imagine why

Grant had returned. Hadn't he told her that he never re-traced his steps?

If she hadn't been so tired, perhaps she would have said nothing. But Emily was tired, and so she blurted out the question that was uppermost in her mind. "Why are you here?"

There was a moment of silence as the question hung between them. Then, to Emily's surprise, Grant shrugged. "I wish I knew." She heard a tentative note in his voice, as if he were as perplexed as she. "I felt as if I had unfinished business here, so I came back."

It was obvious he hadn't wanted to return, and that was yet another surprise for Emily. "I wouldn't have thought you were impulsive." Grant struck her as a man who planned his life and who would let nothing stand between him and accomplishing that plan. That was part of the reason why he had been so frustrated by the automobile's continuing breakdowns.

"Normally I'm not impulsive," he agreed. "I had planned to travel along the coast to Dieppe, but I only got as far as Boulogne-sur-Mer." Grant's jacket rippled as he shrugged his shoulders. "The only way I can describe it is that I felt something pulling me back to Calais."

It couldn't be, she thought, the same magnetism that was even now pulling her closer to him. She was tired. That was all that was wrong with her. Lack of sleep and worry could wreak havoc with a girl's senses. "I'm certain that when the doctors learn you're here, they'll hope you're planning to feature them in one of your columns." Emily was surprised that no one from the hospital staff had come to the garage. Surely by now they'd seen the car and spoken with Robert.

A frown crossed Grant's face, but he extinguished it so quickly that Emily thought she might have imagined it. "Was Dr. Mercer annoyed when I wrote about you?"

A flock of songbirds landed on a chestnut tree near the garage door, the rustling of their wings and their melodic calls loud enough that Emily waited until they were settled before she replied. She shook her head, denying not only the physician's response but also Grant's allegation. "You were writing about ambulance drivers in general," she said.

Grant stretched his hand forward, as if to touch her, then pulled it back. "Emily," he said gently, "I wrote about you. Surely you knew that."

Emily was not a woman who blushed easily, and yet for the second time since Grant had appeared in her garage, her face was suffused with heat. "That's what Sarah said."

"But you didn't believe her." Grant completed the sentence.

"No, I didn't."

He took a step closer. Though he did not touch her, she could feel the heat from his body, and it warmed her more than the coal stove that she used on cold, rainy days.

"That was the point I was making," Grant told her. "You don't take credit for all that you do."

"Everyone knows I repair the ambulances," she countered.

"But you don't advertise your expertise."

"There's a reason why I don't." Emily clenched her fists, wishing for the millionth time that she had not told the officials that she could repair motors. If she hadn't, perhaps they would have sent her closer to the front lines, and perhaps she would already have found Theo. Perhaps she would not be wondering and worrying what he meant by 'my oh.'

"I know better than to ask what that reason is," Grant said. "But I will ask if you'll join me for lunch. I'd like to thank you for fixing Hortense."

Emily stared at Grant. Surely this wasn't the reason he'd returned to Calais. He wouldn't have come all that distance just to invite her to lunch. Of course he hadn't. Hadn't Grant said he couldn't explain why he'd come? It wasn't as if Emily were beautiful like Carolyn. Men would travel long distances to court Carolyn, but Emily wasn't Carolyn, and Grant most definitely was not courting her.

"Have you decided not to replace the car with a horse?" She kept her voice light, reminding herself that it was only because she was tired and worried that she was thinking of courtship.

Grant nodded.

"Then that's all the thanks I need."

"That may be all you need," he said, his voice once again smooth and compelling, "but I have a need to thank you properly."

Emily smiled, thinking of her mother's lessons in etiquette. Though Theo had hated it, he'd been required to learn what their mother called the rules of good breeding along with his sisters. "Your mother must have been a stickler for manners."

A shadow crossed Grant's face, mirroring the shadow that crossed Emily's heart as she thought of Theo lying wounded somewhere here in France. "Something like that," Grant agreed.

For the first time since he'd arrived, Grant did not meet her gaze. That, along with the fleeting expression of pain she had seen on his face, made her sense that he was hiding yet another secret. Like Grant, Emily knew better than to pry, but she also knew that people would often reveal things about themselves when they were relaxed. The prospect of learning more about this man who was unlike anyone she had ever met had her nodding.

"Miss Emily Wentworth accepts Mr. Randall's kind invitation to join him for luncheon." Deliberately, she made her voice and words formal, hoping to coax a smile from him. When it worked, Emily felt a sense of accomplishment as great as when she'd straightened the transmission shaft. Accomplishment mingled with anticipation. There was no doubt that she enjoyed Grant's company. And maybe, just maybe, being with him would help her think about something other than Theo.

Grant pulled out his watch. "Shall we meet in the reception area in an hour?" he asked.

It took Emily only a few minutes to reassemble the ambulance. Though she would normally have taken it for a test drive, she told herself that there would be time to do that when she returned from her appointment with Grant. If she could have carried a tune, Emily imagined she would have been singing as she climbed the stairs to the room she and Sarah shared. As it was, she hummed under her breath, hoping no one heard her tuneless sounds. She couldn't help it, though. For the first time in days, her heart felt light.

It was, she told herself, simply the prospect of a break in her routine. But Emily had never been one for self-deception, and so she admitted that her sense of elation had another source. That source was Grant Randall. There was no denying the fact that he intrigued her. He was a complex man. On the surface, he appeared friendly and open, but there were huge areas that he concealed behind a wall.

Emily had always enjoyed solving puzzles, and she was good at it. That was part of the reason she was frustrated that she had been unable to decipher Theo's message. Perhaps she'd have more success uncovering Grant's secrets.

When she reached her room, Emily poured water into the wash basin and began to clean the dirt and grease from her hands. Minutes later, she pulled a summer frock from her trunk. Today, thank goodness, the sun was shining, and although it was much cooler than it would have been in Texas, the day was warm enough for this dress. Made of a light blue cotton that her sisters had assured her matched her eyes, the dress was one of Emily's favorites. The short

kimono sleeves were comfortable, and the gathered over-
skirt with its patch pocket reminded her of a favorite apron.
But the garment's beauty was the panel at the center of the
bodice. When Martha had sewn the dress, Carolyn had protested that it was too plain and had insisted on embroidering
bluebonnets on the panel. Her sister's handiwork had, Emily admitted, turned an ordinary frock into one she could
wear with pride anywhere.

Emily laid the dress on the bed, then bent at the waist
and began to brush her hair. When it crackled with elec-
tricity, she stood upright and began to arrange it in a chignon. Then she shook her head and swept her hair into a
pompadour. Though the style was years out of date, Emily
knew that it flattered her. And since Grant was at least six
inches taller than she, she need not worry about the extra
height that the more formal hairstyle gave her.

When she entered the large entry hall that served as a
reception area for the hospital, Emily found Grant studying
the map of France and Belgium that dominated one wall.
He turned at the sound of her footsteps on the polished
marble floor and gave her a sweeping bow.

"Your servant, ma'am," Grant said with mock formality.

Emily smiled with pleasure at the obvious admiration in
his gaze. No one at home had looked at her like that. There
all eyes had turned to Carolyn. Young men spoke to Emily,
for they knew that she would understand them. She was
their pal. But Carolyn was the one they courted. Carolyn
was the beautiful Wentworth sister, the one every man in
Canela wanted to marry. Now, for the first time in her life,
someone was looking at her as if she were worth staring
at. It was a heady sensation.

Grant gestured toward the map. "I imagine you have this
memorized."

"Parts of it," she admitted. Like the roads from Calais to

the area of France where Theo's last letters had been posted.

Grant's lips twisted into a frown. "I just heard reports that there's heavy fighting in a new area."

"Where?" The chill that swept through Emily had nothing to do with the cold stone floor beneath her feet. It was the thought of fighting that made her shiver.

Grant pointed to a spot on the map. "It's here, not too far from the town of Maillochauds."

He hadn't shouted. His words were not echoing endlessly. It was only in Emily's imagination that the name of a small French village reverberated. She stared at Grant, not believing she had heard correctly. "My-oh-showed?" she asked, repeating the sound of the town's name.

Emily tried to hide her excitement. Perhaps she was wrong, but she didn't think she was. This was what she had dreamed that Theo had been saying. Maillochauds was where her brother was.

Oblivious to the emotions that raged within her, Grant nodded. "The French would pronounce it a little differently, but you're close."

"My oh . . ." Emily had only one thought, and that was to reach her brother. "I've got to go." She stared at the map for a second, memorizing the location of the town named Maillochauds.

"What's wrong, Emily?"

"I need to go." She moved so quickly that she stumbled as she hurried toward the doorway.

With two steps, Grant was next to her. He slid his arm around her waist. "Come with me." His words brooked no dissent.

"I can't." She had to go to Maillochauds, for that was where Theo was. That was what the dream had meant.

"You're coming with me." Afterwards Emily was not certain how they got there. All she knew was that somehow she and Grant had crossed the courtyard, and he'd persuaded the chef to bring them each a cup of tea. Emily hated tea. It was what her mother made her drink when she was ill. She wasn't ill today; that wasn't the reason her hands were shaking.

"Now, tell me what's wrong." Grant reached across the table and took her hands in his. It was foolish to hope that he wouldn't feel them trembling.

"Believe it or not, Grant, what I just learned was good news."

Grant's expression reflected his skepticism. "Does good news always make you shake like a leaf?"

"I'm not . . ." Emily shrugged. There was no point in denying the obvious. "It's about my brother," she said slowly.

"Theo?" When Emily nodded, Grant's eyes darkened with surprise. "I thought I had heard that he had been killed."

Emily gripped Grant's hands, trying to stop her own from shaking. "That's what the Army thinks," she told him. "But Theo's not dead; I know that."

The chef, who had obviously recognized Grant, approached their table, a plate of pastries in his hand. When Grant had thanked him, he gave Emily an appraising look. "You know your brother's alive because he's your twin." It was a statement, not a question.

"Precisely." Somehow, though others doubted the connection she and Theo shared, Grant did not. "Theo needs me. I'm not sure what's wrong, but I know that he needs me, and I know he's in Maillochauds. I'm going there."

Grant threaded his fingers through hers. "You know you can't do that," he said gently. His eyes held that hint of sorrow that she had glimpsed before. "The Army will never let you go to the front lines."

Emily clenched her teeth. She wouldn't accept that, any

more than she had accepted the Army's other restrictions. "They probably wouldn't have let me come to France if they'd known what I planned to do."

Raising one eyebrow, Grant said, "So that's why you came—to find your brother."

Her secret was out. If Grant told the hospital officials, they might send her back to the States. Emily pulled her hands away from Grant and laid them in her lap. This man held her future in his hands figuratively; she couldn't let him hold her in truth. "Are you going to tell them?"

"And risk having you sabotage Hortense?" Grant's smile was wry. "Hardly! But that doesn't change the fact that you can't go searching for your brother. You know civilians aren't allowed in the battle zone."

"You are."

Grant pushed her teacup toward her and waited until she'd taken a sip before he spoke. "That's true," he admitted.

It didn't matter what the regulations were. It didn't matter what anyone said. Emily was going to find her brother. "If you can go, there must be a way that I can too."

Grant's eyes were filled with compassion. "It's different for you, Emily."

She knew that he was trying to be kind and reasonable, but she didn't want his kindness, nor did she intend to be reasonable. Not when Theo's life was at stake. This was the time to be ruthless and unreasonable.

"Don't you dare tell me I can't go because I'm a woman." Emily leaned across the table to emphasize her point. She had heard that argument far too often. "I've spent my whole life doing the same things Theo did. I played ball with him; he taught me to repair cars; I'd even have gone into battle with him if the Army would have allowed it." As Grant raised an eyebrow, Emily nodded. It was no exaggeration. She would indeed have gone with Theo.

Emily took another sip of tea, trying to calm herself. Though the liquid was bitter, its warmth was soothing. "Grant, my brother needs me," she said, her voice once more steady. "If you won't help me, I'll find another way to get to him. The one thing I won't do is stay here when I know Theo is in Maillochauds."

Grant stared at her for a long moment, his expression once again inscrutable. At length, he said, "All right. I'll see what I can do."

The sun was setting when Grant left the last office. He had accomplished what he'd set out to do. Though the red tape had been more extensive than he'd expected, even given his unusual request, he'd been able to charm, coerce or otherwise convince each of the officials of the importance of his mission. Now, if only he could convince himself!

He was a fool. There was no other way to describe it. Grant quickened his pace. Perhaps that would help dissipate the feeling that he had made a huge mistake. You would have thought he would have learned this particular lesson years ago. Hadn't he learned anything after what happened with Carl and Mickey? Grant had been only a child when he had vowed never to let himself care deeply about another human being. He'd kept that vow, and had even extended it beyond the human race. For only months after Mickey left, Grant had found Augustus.

The little mutt had been nameless until Grant had adopted him. He wasn't a regal animal. Far from it. But surely a dog who'd been named after a Roman emperor would be more powerful than Mrs. Schiller. Surely she wouldn't . . . Grant swallowed deeply. He wouldn't think about that. It was long past, and he couldn't undo what had happened that day. All Grant could do—all he had done—was to make sure that he never again became attached to either people or animals.

Until today. Today proved that, no matter how well he thought he had learned the lessons of his childhood, he still had more to learn.

Dr. Mercer and one of the other physicians stood in the doorway of the small room they'd turned into a staff lounge. It was here, Grant knew, that they played cards and told stories to help them forget, if only briefly, the horrors that they dealt with in the operating theater. When the doctors saw Grant, they beckoned to him to join them. He shook his head. Tonight he wanted no one's company, not even his own.

He couldn't explain why he had felt compelled to come back to Calais. As he had told Emily, there had been something drawing him to this city. And when he'd seen her smile as he entered the garage, Grant had known that it was right that he'd returned. There was something different about Emily, something special. That was why when he had heard her story, though he'd known he ought to refuse, he hadn't.

Emily Wentworth was a woman with a mission, and Grant admired that. It didn't seem to matter that she was like Don Quixote, tilting at windmills, for how else could you describe her plan to go behind enemy lines and rescue her brother?

Grant frowned. If she was Don Quixote, did that make him Sancho Panza, the faithful sidekick? It didn't matter. He'd been called worse. What mattered was that he knew he had to help her, no matter how quixotic her goal. And so he'd met with the Army, persuading them that he needed to see this latest fighting. When they were convinced, he'd spoken to the hospital administrator, explaining that he needed a driver to take him to the front lines and asking for Emily. The administrator hadn't wanted to agree. It was, he pointed out, highly irregular. But Grant had argued that he needed not just a skilled driver but also one who could fix the automobile. His life might depend on having a running motor. Grudgingly, the man had agreed. Now all that remained was to tell Emily.

As Grant had hoped, when he approached the garage, there was a light on inside. Emily was working late. He slid the door open and called her name.

"Grant?" The clank of metal on stone told him she'd dropped her tool in her eagerness to see him. He was a fool to be doing this, but he'd be an even greater fool to disappoint Emily Wentworth.

"We're going to Maillochauds," he said.

The blood drained from her face, and for a second, Grant was afraid she would faint. "It's all right, Emily," he said, holding out his hands to her. "I told them I needed you, and they agreed."

As his words registered, Emily's lips turned up. "Oh, Grant," she said, her voice cracking with emotion.

Only once before had Grant seen a person literally glowing with happiness. The last time it had been Christmas morning, nearly 20 years earlier. That day Grant had watched as Mickey wakened. The boy's eyes had flown open, and there had been a second of fear. Then when he'd seen a bulge in the stocking hanging at the foot of his bed, Mickey's smile had threatened to crack his face, and his eyes had glowed with the same light that Emily's did today. The other boys had ridiculed Mickey, telling him there was no Santa Claus, but Mickey had insisted on hanging his best stocking. He had believed in the legend, and the next morning he had proof. Only Grant knew the truth.

"Really truly?" Emily asked, jolting Grant back to the present.

"Really truly."

That beautiful face glowed with happiness. "Oh, Grant! Thank you! You won't regret this."

Grant wasn't so sure.

Chapter Five

Naturally it was raining when Hortense broke down. Emily wasn't surprised by the timing. After all, in this part of France, days without rain were rare, and despite Grant's confidence in her ability to repair cars, Hortense did seem to be more prone to breakdowns than any other flivver Emily had seen. Even Gertie, the hospital's ambulance, was reliable compared to Grant's vehicle.

"How bad is it this time?" Grant asked even before Emily climbed out of the automobile. The frequency of Hortense's mechanical problems had led them to develop a game, guessing what was wrong and how long the delay would be.

Emily reached into the back seat and pulled out her sou'wester. Though she frequently had to roll up the sleeves to work on the car, the broad brimmed hat kept rain from trickling down her neck, and that helped, even if only marginally. It was, she had discovered, far more difficult to repair a vehicle in the rain than it had been to work on Gertie and Lucille in the garage.

Still, even though the delays were frustrating, Emily was happier than she'd been since she left Texas. Now she knew where Theo was, and she was on her way to him. Thanks to Grant. Though she doubted he'd appreciate the term, Grant had been her silver lining on that awful day when she'd despaired of finding her brother. It was Grant's casual comment that had revealed the name of the village where Emily believed Theo was living, and Grant who had found a way for her to go there with the Army's blessing.

"I'm afraid Hortense wants a rest." Emily settled the hat on her head and stepped down from the car. Though the roads were so badly rutted that she had feared an especially deep rut would cause a broken spring, this time there was no doubt that something was wrong with the motor. The snapping sound she'd heard a second before the Model T stopped could mean only one thing: a broken fan belt. Emily opened the hood and confirmed her diagnosis.

"I don't like the sound of that. It's only a few syllables from 'rest' to 'final resting place.' "

Emily turned to stare at Grant. "When I first met you, I thought that's what you wanted—the end of Hortense. As I recall, you thought a horse would be more reliable."

Grant shrugged. "Maybe I've changed my mind." He shrugged again, as if uncomfortable with the conversation. "If I did, it's your fault."

Emily couldn't help it. She grinned. "Then I've accomplished something good."

"And as your reward," Grant said, returning her smile, "you have the privilege of repairing Hortense yet another time."

Suddenly Emily didn't mind either the rain or Hortense's propensity to break down. What mattered was the fact that Grant was smiling. He stood at her side and peered at the engine, as if he could somehow reverse the damage. Emily wasn't certain whether Grant was trying to learn something about the car, perhaps a few facts he could include in a future column, or whether he was merely being polite. Neither would have surprised Emily. What did surprise her was her reaction to having Grant so close.

In the past, she had preferred to work alone. Observers, Emily had learned, often distracted her with their questions and suggestions. But Grant was different. He seemed to know when she was concentrating and did not interrupt then. On the other hand, when she was performing purely mechanical tasks, she welcomed his companionship. Though he avoided any discussions of his own past, Grant was a skilled observer and would regale her with details of the countryside she had missed. Traveling with Grant had shown Emily aspects of France that she doubted very many others had seen, and that was yet another silver lining.

"We're lucky this time," she said.

As Emily had expected, he frowned. "We're stopped at the side of a mud-soaked road. Our vehicle has a broken fan belt. It's raining so hard that I can hardly see. And you're telling me that we're lucky. Are you some kind of Pollyanna?"

"I've been accused of that," Emily admitted. She held up her hand, her fingers fisted. "First of all," she said, unfolding her index finger, "I have a spare fan belt. Secondly," the middle finger, "we're not too far from a town." They were traveling southeast from Calais, following secondary roads rather than risking an encounter with the enemy on the main road. Though the secondary roads were in even worse condition than the primary ones, Grant had insisted on taking the precaution. "And thirdly," Emily continued, raising her ring finger, "that means you'll have time to buy us some food while I fix the car."

Grant made a noise that might have been a chuckle. When he spoke, though, his voice was solemn. Grant wasn't one for finding humor in their predicaments. "If I subscribe to your philosophy," he said, "I'm supposed to be happy because Hortense broke down and now I can walk

through the rain to buy food when, if this piece of auto-
motive wonder had continued running, we could have
driven into the town."

Emily shook her head. "You know we wouldn't have
driven, anyway."

They had been careful to park Hortense where she would
not be easily seen and had walked into the few towns that
they'd visited. It was another of Grant's precautions. Two
Americans were conspicuous enough. Combine them with
Henry Ford's invention, and no one would forget that
they'd been there. Had it not been wartime, they would not
have been so cautious. Of course, had it not been wartime,
neither of them would have been here. Emily would have
been home in Canela, and Grant . . . She wondered what
Grant would have been doing. Since he never spoke of the
past, it was almost as if his life had begun when he'd come
to France as a journalist. Emily knew that wasn't possible,
but the man was so secretive that it was difficult to picture
him anywhere other than here.

"How can you be so optimistic?" Grant asked. Though
his words were light, Emily detected a note of puzzlement
in his voice.

"Each mile brings me closer to Theo. That's what's important," she told Grant. And it was. Nothing else mattered,
not the rain, not the car's propensity to break down, nothing. All that mattered was finding her brother. That's why
they were headed toward St. Omer and Arras. Maillochauds
was less than 30 miles—50 kilometers—north of Arras.
And Theo was in Maillochauds. Emily was certain of that.

From the corner of her eye, Emily saw something move.
She turned, then smiled. "If I'm not mistaken, you'll soon
have company on your walk."

An elderly Frenchman was approaching. Though the rain
had intensified, he walked slowly, as if taking a stroll in
the park, apparently oblivious to the downpour. Somehow

the jaunty angle of the man's beret seemed at odds with his deliberate pace and the pipe clenched between his teeth.

"Morning." The man greeted Grant. His black suit was a decade out of fashion, a fact that appeared to bother the man not a whit more than the rain that soaked through the wool. "It 'pears you've got yourself some trouble." Emily continued threading the fan belt around the pulleys. It wasn't the first time a man had spoken to Grant, nor was it the first time one had acted as if she were invisible.

"Nothing this woman can't fix."

"Her?" The man came closer. Though Emily looked up and smiled at the man, she noticed that he did not meet her gaze.

Grant nodded and clapped the man on the shoulder. "She's the best. Better at this than any man I've ever met."

This time the farmer stared at her. Slowly, he removed his beret in greeting. "*Bonjour, madame.*" Then he turned back to Grant. "I never heard of a woman working on one of those things." He gestured toward Hortense with his pipe.

Grant gave the man an appraising look. "Now, sir, I imagine you've seen stranger things than this."

With all thoughts of buying food apparently forgotten, Grant began to draw out the older man. Though the rain continued, blurring Grant's glasses and extinguishing the man's pipe, the two of them stood a few yards away from Emily, seemingly oblivious to the weather, as the Frenchman told Grant about the pilot whose plane had crashed in a nearby field. Though the man was hesitant at first, Grant's skillful questions encouraged him to recount not only the drama of the downed pilot but also the way the neighboring farmers had conspired to hide the plane from the enemy.

It was, Emily reflected, a measure of Grant's talent that the man appeared to have no idea he was being interviewed. Instead, the conversation flowed as smoothly as if they were friends of long standing, catching up on what had happened in their lives while they were apart. The Frenchman spoke slowly and deliberately, choosing his words carefully, but the picture he painted was a vivid one. For his part, though Grant related several anecdotes which purported to be part of his past, Emily doubted their veracity. There was something in his tone that told her he was inventing the story of his family's visit to a farm and that he had chosen the tale merely to encourage this farmer to share more of his stories.

She tightened the clamp on the fan belt, checked it one last time, then straightened her back, easing the cramp that bending over the engine always caused.

"Finished?" Grant took a step closer and peered inside the hood. It was, Emily suspected, like his fabricated tales, an action designed to inspire confidence in the farmer. The man would expect Grant, another male, to know how the motor worked.

Emily nodded. Hortense was as ready as she would ever be. With the new fan belt, the engine would once again run. How long remained to be seen.

The farmer appeared suitably impressed when Grant turned the starting crank and the motor began to clank. "Very good, *monsieur*." There was no disguising the admiration in his voice. "Would you and *madame* wish to share *le déjeuner* with my wife and me?"

Grant gave Emily a quick glance. The Frenchman, she was certain, did not realize that Grant was asking whether Emily wanted to join the farmer and his wife for dinner and that if she was unwilling, Grant would politely decline the invitation. Emily nodded almost imperceptibly.

"You are most kind, *monsieur*," Grant said smoothly. "We would be honored, if we are not imposing on your hospitality."

"But no," the farmer protested. "It is not often we have visitors from America."

Emily hoped his wife would be as understanding when two unexpected guests arrived for the noon meal. She had seen enough of the French countryside to know that food was in short supply. While no one on farms appeared to be starving, there was no doubt that rations were limited.

When they reached the small stone farmhouse, Emily and Grant remained outside while the farmer, who had told them his name was Monsieur Ferrand, advised his wife of their guests' arrival. Less than a minute later, he returned, a petite woman at his side. Like many French women, Madame Ferrand was dressed all in black, and her gray hair was pulled back into a knot.

"*Bienvenue chez nous*," the woman said, her thin face breaking into a smile as she welcomed them to her home. "I hope you will excuse our simple fare."

Though her French was rudimentary, Emily assured the woman that she and Grant were delighted to have been invited. "Something smells delicious," she said truthfully.

The scent of chicken broth and fragrant vegetables filled the small room that appeared to serve as the family's primary living quarters. A table for six filled one half of the room, while a settee and two comfortable chairs flanked a gas stove on the other side of the room. Emily guessed that the kitchen was behind the door closest to the table and that the other door led to the couple's bedroom.

With its whitewashed walls and stone floor, the house was far smaller and simpler than the one where Emily had grown up, and yet she felt the same warmth that had surrounded her during her childhood. This was a house filled with love. It was apparent in the way the couple looked at each other, the fond smiles they gave each other, the occasional touches. Though they had been married for more than half a century, a fact Grant quickly extracted from

Madame Ferrand, they acted more like newlyweds than Emily's sister Martha and her husband had during the first year of their marriage.

"Please, please, be seated." Madame Ferrand urged Emily to take the seat at her right, placing Grant on her left. As she served bowls of what she called a simple *potage* accompanied by a fat loaf of crusty bread, the French-woman continued to apologize for the meal. "Had I known, I could have killed a chicken." She smoothed the oilcloth tablecloth, expressing her regret that she had no linens.

Emily shook her head. "I cannot imagine anything tasting more delicious than this." The *potage*, as Madame Ferrand called her soup, might have been made of simple ingredients—nothing more than chicken broth, vegetables and a few herbs, she claimed—but the combination surpassed anything Emily had eaten at the Canela Country Club. She smiled, wondering whether her sister Carolyn would return to work at the country club when the war was over and whether Emily could persuade the chef to try French chicken soup.

"My wife is a very good cook, is she not?" the French-man asked, his eyes lingering on his wife's face.

"She is the best," Emily agreed.

"And you, *monsieur*, are the most gracious of hosts." As Grant praised the man, his wife's eyes lit with pride.

"See, Ferrand, I told you so. I am fortunate to have you." Madame Ferrand gave her husband a smile that could only be described as coquettish. It should have looked silly on a woman of her age, and yet it did not. Instead, it turned the woman's face from plain to beautiful and made her husband glow with pleasure.

This was love, true love, the kind that lasted through the ages. The sight of the Ferrands' happiness, despite the two children they had buried—another story Grant had managed to learn without seeming to ask—filled Emily's heart with joy. It reaffirmed her belief in happy endings and in the power of love. Yet at the same time that she rejoiced for this couple, Emily found herself overcome with an almost unbearable sense of longing. This was what she wanted, to love and be loved. But love was elusive. Love wasn't something you learned, like catching a ball or repairing an engine. It was a gift, a wonderful gift, and not everyone received it. Emily had seen enough married couples to know that what her parents and the Ferrands shared was special. Though happiness like theirs was rare, it was what Emily sought. What wrenched her heart was the fear that she might never find it.

When the meal was over, both Grant and Emily tried to find a way to repay their hosts' kindness. It was obvious that the couple was far from wealthy and that by sharing their dinner with strangers, they would in all likelihood have nothing more than bread for the next day's meal. It was also obvious that offering them money would be an insult. Emily resolved that when she returned home, as soon as this horrible war was ended, she would send the Ferrands a box of pecans from the trees in her backyard along with the other ingredients for pecan pie. The nuts, she had learned, were virtually unknown in Europe, and Madame Ferrand had appeared interested in the Southern delicacy. But that was in the future. Emily wished there were something she could do today.

The rain had begun to ease, and now only a light mist fell. Though both Grant and Emily urged the Ferrands to remain inside, their hosts insisted on accompanying them back to the automobile. It was when she saw Madame Ferrand's inquisitive expression that Emily realized what she could do.

"Would you like a ride?" she offered.

The older couple exchanged glances, then looked at

Grant, as if seeking his approval. He nodded. "Emily is a first rate driver," he announced. "You're in for a treat."

Though Grant suggested that the Ferrands sit in the front, claiming that they would have a better view there, Emily shook her head. One of the disadvantages of the earlier Model T's, including the 1911 cars, was that the front compartment was open on the sides. Though the absence of doors made it easy to climb in and out, on a rainy day it meant that occupants became wet and all too often muddy. The rear compartment, or tonneau as it was sometimes called, was drier.

Emily opened the door and helped the older couple climb into Hortense. A minute later they were in motion. Emily doubted that either of the Ferrands looked through the windshield. Instead, they held hands and stared out the side window, as if mesmerized by the speed with which they were passing their own fields. "*Merveilleux!*" Madame Ferrand whispered. Yes, it was marvelous, Emily thought, remembering her own first ride. The road was rutted and mud spattered the side of the car as they lurched along the lane. Hortense's motor sputtered a little as it always did when first started. The road was so narrow that the automobile barely cleared the hedges on either side. These were not ideal conditions for a ride, and yet there was no doubt that the Ferrands were enjoying it.

"*Merci bien,*" Monsieur Ferrand said, his voice shaking ever so slightly as he helped his wife from the car at the end of the ride. "*Au revoir.*"

Emily hoped she would see them again. But even if she did not, she knew that this was a day she would not forget. She and Grant had spent no more than two hours in the Ferrands' company, but during those hours Emily had been able to forget that there was a war raging only miles away. The love that the Ferrands shared was so strong that it had enfolded Emily and Grant, giving them a respite from reality.

"Am I right in guessing that you'll write a column about the effects of war on one ordinary French couple?" Emily asked Grant when they were once more headed south.

He nodded as he polished his spectacles. "I hadn't realized I was so transparent. But, yes, you're right. I found them refreshing. Somehow, although they're close to the fighting, they seem to have created an oasis of tranquility and peace." He had felt it, too, but—being Grant—he'd been able to express his thoughts far more eloquently than Emily.

"I thought they were charming," Emily smiled, remembering how the Ferrands had gazed at each other. "It's wonderful to see a couple still in love after so many years."

They had reached a crossroads without a sign, one of the disadvantages of traveling on unmarked roads. Emily looked in both directions, trying to determine which way they should turn. Hortense had enough gas to reach the next town, but only if they made the correct turn. Normally Emily would have judged direction by the sun. Unfortunately, today there was no sun. Then she spotted what appeared to be a white tombstone at the side of the road. The letters painted on it stated that it was 10 kilometers to Moulie, and Moulie was the direction they wanted to go.

"I imagine you've been in love a dozen times."

Emily stared at Grant, astonished by his statement. Whatever made him think that she would have been in love? "I'm afraid not."

"Eleven times, then." The man was persistent. Emily knew that from the conversations he had had with Monsieur Ferrand. When he didn't get an answer to his question, Grant would find another way to phrase it. The result was that people he interviewed frequently revealed far more than Emily suspected they had intended to. He wasn't interviewing her. Emily knew that. But for some reason, Grant wanted to discuss love. Unfortunately, it was not a topic Emily wanted to discuss, particularly not today when she had seen true love and realized how very much she wanted to experience it.

"Never." Surely Grant would realize that she was dodging his question the way he did so many of hers. Surely he would change the subject.

"I don't believe that."

Emily slowed the car and turned to look at Grant. "I've told you about my family. Carolyn is the beautiful one. She's the Wentworth daughter the boys wanted to marry." The truth was, no one in Canela had ever paid much attention to Emily. Martha had been lucky. She had married Henry before Carolyn was old enough to be courted. But once Carolyn was of marriageable age, every young man in Canela and the surrounding region had made his way to the Wentworth home. As long as Carolyn had remained unmarried, the bachelors of Canela had remained hopeful, and Emily had remained alone, unable and unwilling to compete with her sister's beauty.

"The boys must have been blind."

It was a kind thought, if an inaccurate one. The truth was, Emily hadn't spent a lot of time dreaming about love. She and Theo had discussed it, just as they'd discussed the possibility of building houses next to each other. But falling in love and building houses had always been in the future.

"I'm not sure how Theo would have reacted to someone courting me," Emily said lightly.

"Was he protective?"

She shook her head. "That's the wrong word." Their father had been protective of Martha. Theo wasn't like that. "We're so much a part of each other that it's difficult being separated." That was part of what made this war so horrible. "Theo and I always said we'd have to marry twins, because no one else would understand the link we share."

Grant nodded as he pushed his glasses back onto his nose. "I've talked to other twins, and they say the same thing."

The road veered to the left. As she depressed the clutch to slow Hortense, Emily gasped. Instead of being filled with newly sprouting crops, the farmlands ahead of them were blackened and pocked with large craters.

"Shelling," Grant confirmed. "You wouldn't think crops would burn when there's this much rain, but they do." His lips tightened, and Emily guessed he was thinking, as she was, of the misery the farmers would endure if they could not replant.

"Tell me about Theo," Grant said, clearly trying to steer Emily's thoughts away from the destruction.

"I'm close to my sisters," she admitted, "but it's not the same as what Theo and I share."

"I wouldn't know about that."

Though Grant's words were simple, his tone held a bleakness that surprised Emily. "I can't imagine growing up without siblings. You must have been lonely." Ed Bleeker, the Wentworths' next door neighbor, had been an only child, but he hadn't seemed lonely.

Grant's face took on that shuttered look Emily had seen so often. "I wasn't alone."

"Of course not. You had your parents." But that couldn't have been the same as having sisters and a brother. Ed, Emily remembered, had spent so much time at her house that he'd been close to an honorary brother.

"How far are we from Moulie?" Grant changed the subject. Emily shouldn't have been surprised. He did that every time the conversation turned to himself. What she didn't understand was why he was so unwilling to talk about his past.

Grant Randall was an enigma. Although he was undeniably skilled at drawing stories from other people and
making them believe that he cared about them, he often
seemed aloof, as if he were simply observing life from a
distance. Emily had seen the wall that he erected when she
had asked him to hold the injured kitten. At the time, she
had thought Grant was simply shielding himself from pain.
But it appeared that he built the same barricade against
happiness, and that made no sense. Why would anyone iso-
late himself from joy? Something in Grant's past had made
him that way, but Emily was no closer to learning what it
was than she had been the first day she met him. Grant
Randall was a puzzle, and thus far Emily had failed mis-
erably at solving it.

*It was Christmas night. The cold rain had turned to
snow, and the ground was covered in white. Grant winked
at Mickey, giving him their secret signal, then slipped out
of the house and headed for the stable. Mrs. Schiller would
be angry if she discovered that they'd gone outside. It was
a risk they'd have to take. Normally Grant wouldn't have
subjected Mickey to Mrs. Schiller's possible wrath, but he
figured that by morning, the snow would have covered their
footprints, and she'd never know.*

*"You was right!" Mickey's voice brimmed with excite-
ment as he grabbed Grant's arm. "Santa came!" Though
the stable was dark, the reflection of the moon on snow was
bright enough that Grant could see the sparks in Mickey's
eyes.*

*"That's 'cause you're special," Grant told the younger
boy. Grant had long since known that there was no Santa,
but—despite the other boys' teasing—Mickey believed in
things like goodness and red-suited men who brought pres-
ents at Christmas. That was why Grant had taken the
chances he had. First he'd entered the forbidden territory*

of the kitchen. Then he'd stolen the fig. And then he'd made sure that Mickey wakened before the others so that no one would take the boy's treat from him.

"Look, Grant." Mickey held out the dried fig that he'd discovered in his sock that morning. *"It's my present from Santa."*

Grant's heart swelled with happiness at the young boy's pleasure. *"You're supposed to eat it,"* he said. Grant had whispered that admonition to Mickey that morning when the boy had pulled the fruit from his stocking and had believed that Mickey had long since consumed the treat.

"I wanted to share it with you."

Grant squeezed his eyes shut. Those weren't tears. Big boys didn't cry. *"Oh, Mickey. It's yours."*

The boy shook his head. *"It'll taste better if we share it."* He broke the fruit and handed Grant a piece. *"You first,"* he said.

Though his throat had a lump bigger than the turkey Mrs. Schiller had served them, somehow Grant managed to swallow the fig. He'd made a ceremony of chewing it, then, when he'd extracted every last bit of flavor, he'd swallowed. Grant didn't think he'd ever tasted anything as delicious as that morsel of dried fruit. It wasn't that it was forbidden fruit. Grant knew some of the boys claimed that food tasted better when they'd pilfered it from the kitchen, but Grant had never believed that. It wasn't that he especially liked figs. He didn't. What made this one so savory was the fact that Mickey had given it to him.

The boy had no way of knowing that Grant and not Santa had put the fig in his stocking. He believed a jolly old man in a red suit had paid a special visit to the orphanage and that he'd left Mickey a gift. And Mickey had shared that special treat with Grant. Grant blinked his eyes again.

"You know what I wish?" Mickey asked when he'd swallowed.

Grant shook his head. Mickey had wished for Santa Claus, and Grant had made that dream come true. What did he want now?

"I wish you were my brother."

One of the horses whinnied, as if he approved. "Me too." When Carl had left, Grant had believed that he would never have another friend. Carl had been the only one who talked to him, the only one who didn't laugh when he couldn't read the teacher's writing on the blackboard. But then Carl had gone, and Grant had been alone again.

It had seemed like forever until one day Mickey had joined the boys at the dinner table, taking a seat across from Grant. Boys came and went, but none had looked at Grant the way Mickey did. The newcomer was younger than Grant and smaller than the other boys his age. Grant knew what that meant. The others would bully Mickey. Unless someone looked out for him. Mickey knew it too. There was a wariness to him that told Grant he knew what would happen when the lights went out. When Mickey looked at Grant, Grant saw his own fears reflected. He remembered how lonely the first months here were. He remembered how much he had hated the orphanage until Carl had befriended him. And in that moment when their eyes met, Grant knew that he couldn't let this boy suffer the way he had. Mickey wasn't his brother, but if he could have chosen one, Grant would have picked him.

"Let's pretend," he said.

Mickey jumped up from the bale of hay and tugged on Grant's arm. "Can't you adopt me?" he demanded. "Then we'd always be together."

With the wisdom of his eight years, Grant ruffled Mickey's hair. "Silly. One of us can't adopt another." He only wished he could. Even better, he wished he were old enough to run away and to take Mickey with him.

"I thought you could do anything." The disappointment

in Mickey's voice was almost more than Grant could bear. How he wished he were as powerful as the young boy believed. It was one thing to put a fig in a sock. This was much more difficult.

Grant thought for a long moment. There had to be something he could do to keep Mickey's Christmas special. "I read about something that'll make us real brothers," he said at last. "They call it blood brothers." Grant explained what was involved. "Are you brave enough?"

Mickey nodded. "I'd do anything to be your brother."

Ten minutes later, holding their fingers in the air to stop the bleeding, the boys grinned at each other. "We're brothers now," Grant told Mickey. "Nothing can separate us."

But one afternoon before the crocuses bloomed, Grant saw a strange carriage stop in front of the building and a couple in fancy clothing get out of it. He knew what that meant. The man and lady wanted to adopt a boy. Not him, of course. Mrs. Schiller had told him that no one wanted a boy who couldn't see right. Who was the lucky boy?

Grant hid behind the hedge, waiting to see who came out. The man came first, then the woman, then . . . No! It couldn't be!

"I don't want to go!" Tears streamed down Mickey's face, and he tugged on the woman's hand, trying to get away. "My brother's here!"

Mrs. Schiller frowned. "Pay no attention to him," she told the woman and her husband. "He has no brothers."

Mickey kicked at the man's leg. "I do so," he cried. "Grant's my brother!"

Mrs. Schiller turned to the man. "Don't worry. He'll soon forget."

But Grant had not.

Chapter Six

"Look, Grant. Isn't that the silliest bird you've ever seen?"

As the bird in question flew from the hedgerow, its wings fluttering, its beak opening and closing rapidly as it chirped to another unseen bird, Emily turned to the man in the passenger seat. Surely he would have found the bird's antics amusing. First, it had rolled in the mud, perhaps mistaking the brown substance for the dustbath she knew birds craved. Then it had peered at its mud-caked wings with what appeared to be disgust before preening. And then, when its wings were once more clean, it had begun to flit from one side of the road to the other, perching on the hedgerows as it announced its arrival to the other birds.

Grant merely shrugged. "If you ask me, all birds are silly."

The uncharacteristically cynical response confirmed what Emily had feared. Something was bothering Grant. She looked at him, trying to guess what was wrong. The man was almost unfairly handsome, even at the end of the day when he was tired and unshaven. This early in the morning, his hair still damp, a small nick on his cheek betraying the haste with which he'd shaved, he was positively magnificent. But, though Grant was as handsome as ever, there was no ignoring the fact that he also appeared tired. Emily knew why she was tired. She had been worried about Theo. But surely Grant had no reason to worry. It must be something else that had kept him from sleeping.

"Did you finish your column last night?" Emily asked. He had mentioned once that when he was excited by his subject, he would write until the column was finished, no matter how late that might be. In all probability that was what he had been doing last night, and that was the reason fatigue lined his face. It wasn't worry.

Grant nodded. "I finished the first one."

"The first?"

He nodded again. "The Ferrands were a real inspiration. I got ideas for at least three stories."

A weight Emily hadn't known she had been carrying was lifted. "I'm so glad," she said. "Sometimes I feel guilty that you're going to Maillochauds when you'd rather be somewhere else."

Grant looked as if she had surprised him. "You shouldn't feel guilty. One thing I've learned is that I can find ideas almost anywhere. A detour in the road could lead to one of my best columns." He gave the dashboard an almost affectionate pat. "Look what happened when Hortense broke down near the Ferrands' farm."

Emily felt her spirits rise another notch. "I was afraid that you were worried about something."

A shadow crossed Grant's face. "I used to think I was good at hiding my feelings," he said, "but you seem to have more than your share of intuition." Grant stared at the road for a moment, his indecision obvious. "Emily, you know I'm a writer," he said at last. "Part of being a writer means looking for answers and asking difficult questions."

Emily nodded. She had watched him do exactly that,

probing for the reason behind someone's response. What she didn't know was what particular question was bothering him. Emily thought quickly, trying to remember anything the Ferrands might have said that would have disturbed Grant. "What is it?" she asked when she could find no obvious cause for his uneasiness.

Grant waited until they'd rounded the bend in the road before he said, "It's your brother."

"Theo?"

Grant's smile was wry. "As far as I know, he's the only one you have." His face once more somber, Grant continued, "I don't understand why he hasn't contacted anyone. It's been weeks since his battalion was attacked. Surely by now if he's in Maillochauds, someone would have notified the Army."

Emily nodded slowly. "I've asked myself the same question," she admitted. "It must be that Theo can't tell people where he is. Maybe he's too badly wounded, or maybe he has amnesia. I heard one of the doctors in Calais say that sometimes men who've gone through horrible experiences don't remember who they are."

When Grant looked skeptical, Emily said, "The alternative is simply not possible." Her brother was alive; she knew it.

Grant pushed his glasses back onto his nose, then touched the bump where it had been broken. "I don't know how you do it, Emily, but you're the most optimistic person I've ever met. You really are a Pollyanna."

"My sisters claimed that Eleanor Porter modeled her heroine on me."

"You mean you play the 'glad game?'" Grant asked, referring to the fictional Pollyanna's insistence that there was something to be glad about in every situation.

Emily shrugged. "I didn't call it that. My mother claimed

that ever since I was a small child, I looked for silver linings."

Grant stared at the clear blue sky. "I don't see any clouds today. So, tell me, Miss Emily Who Isn't Pollyanna, how do you find a silver lining today?"

Feigning annoyance, Emily said, "You of all people should know that that was figurative. The point is to find something good in every day."

"It's an interesting theory. I think I could be convinced to be optimistic—maybe I could even believe in miracles—if Hortense went a week without a breakdown."

As if on cue, there was a sputter, and the automobile coasted to a stop.

Emily shook her finger at Grant. "It's your fault," she said, pretending to be angry. The truth was, she couldn't be angry with this man who had brought her so many silver linings.

Grant heard the mirth in her voice and responded in kind, feigning regret. "I won't tempt fate again," he said, his voice a parody of a naughty child's. "I promise."

When Emily opened the hood, though Grant took his usual spot at her side, Emily sensed his impatience. "It shouldn't take too long to fix—half an hour or so. All that's wrong is that the radiator inlet hose slipped off."

Grant nodded. Most repairs required between half an hour and an hour. "If you don't mind, I'll take advantage of the time to start my next column," he told her and reached for his camp stool.

Though Emily regretted every breakdown, since each one delayed their arrival in Maillochauds, she was thankful for today's sunshine. It was easier—not to mention more pleasant—to work on Hortense when the sun was out. And, fortunately, this repair was one of the easier ones. Emily reached into the engine and tugged the hose back into place. There. All that was left was to tighten the clamps.

They'd be back on the road in less time than she had expected.

She was tightening the last clamp when it happened. A cloud crossed the sun, and for a second Emily felt as if she had been plunged into darkness. Even a cloudy, moonless night was not this dark. Even the time she had played hide-and-seek and had hidden inside mother's cedar chest had not been this dark.

Theo! Emily gripped the edge of the car, trying to keep from falling. Though it was totally irrational, she feared that something had happened to her brother. There was no reason to feel this way. The sun was still shining. Grant was sitting on the blanket, scribbling on a piece of paper as though nothing unusual had happened. A cloud had covered the sun for an instant. That was all. It was simply her imagination that had magnified the momentary shadow, turning it into something sinister. But, try though she might, Emily could not dismiss her uneasiness and her sense that something was wrong with Theo. There was no silver lining in this cloud.

Emily forced herself to take a deep breath as she tried to quell her fears. Theo wasn't dead. She took another deep breath and exhaled slowly. *Be sensible*, she told herself. *Worry will accomplish nothing. What you need to do is find Theo—quickly.* She and Grant would be in Maillochauds in less than a week, and then Emily could see for herself what Theo needed. But what if she was too late?

She wouldn't be. She couldn't be!

The words were flowing easily today. Grant hated both the days when he had to struggle to find the correct word and the ones when his ideas felt as stale as three-day-old bread. Today, thank goodness, was not one of those days. Today his pen could barely keep up with his thoughts, and he found himself scribbling only the first few letters of words, hoping he would be able to transcribe them later.

He was halfway through his column when he heard the cry. His own heart beating as fast as a cornered rabbit's, Grant jumped to his feet and raced toward the car.

"Emily! What's wrong?" She stood in front of Hortense, her hands gripping the metal as if the automobile were somehow a lifeline. Grant looked around. There was no sign of blood nor anything that might have injured Emily. "Emily." He laid his hand on hers, hoping to comfort her. "What's the matter?"

"Please, Grant." Her voice was faint, and she enunciated each word carefully, as if she were speaking a foreign language. "I don't want to talk about it."

Grant nodded. If there was one thing he understood, it was the desire not to put fears into words. Sometimes, the action of voicing them made them more real. It was easier to deny them if they were never spoken.

"All right," he agreed. If Emily wanted to pretend that nothing was wrong, he could play that game, at least for a while. He looked at the car. "Is Hortense fixed?" When Emily nodded, Grant lifted his hand from hers. "That's good news, because I'm ready for dinner."

Emily closed the hood. "Would you mind if we bought some food and had a picnic?" Before Grant had a chance to reply, she added, "It's too nice a day to stay inside."

Though Grant had been looking forward to a hot meal, he agreed. Emily didn't care about the weather. He was certain of that. But he was also certain that she had a reason for wanting to eat quickly and that that reason was connected to her obvious fear.

"That's a wonderful idea, Miss Sunshine." Grant forced a lightness he didn't feel into his voice. Emily needed comfort, and the only comfort he knew to give her was the pretense that nothing was wrong.

Half an hour later when they had spread the car robe on the ground and were seated on it, eating bread and cheese, Grant could almost believe that nothing was wrong. It was a beautiful day. The sun shone from a faultlessly blue sky; songbirds warbled in the poplars; the scent of spring flowers filled the air. At this moment, it was difficult to believe that men were fighting just a few miles away. Grant and Emily could have been any man and woman enjoying a pastoral picnic, if only Emily weren't so distraught. Though she tried to mask it, her hands still trembled, and although some color had returned to her cheeks, her eyes still held that haunted look.

Grant wished there were something he could do to erase the shadows and make Emily smile again. To do that, though, meant confronting her fears. Grant would not do that. She had asked for privacy, and he would honor her request. But, oh, how he wished he had it in his power to turn back time and to ensure that nothing marred Emily Wentworth's day.

Emily had once said she felt guilty about taking Grant so far from his original destination. What she didn't know and what Grant wouldn't tell her was how much he had enjoyed their journey and how often he regretted that he could do so little. He couldn't repair Hortense, and he didn't even dare drive the car, lest he take them into a ditch. While the trip to Maillochauds might have started as Emily's quest, it had become the single most memorable journey Grant had ever taken.

The last telegram he had received from his editor had confirmed what Grant had thought: the columns he had written since he'd left Calais were the best he had done. Emily was more than his driver, more even than the impetus for the trip. She was the catalyst. Grant knew that, and he wished there were some way he could repay her for all that she had done for him.

When they arrived in the town where they had agreed they would stop for the day, Grant gestured toward the one inn. "It looks reasonably clean. I'll see if they have room for us."

Emily shook her head, and once more her expression was pleading. "Let's go to the next town. It's only another hour."

Grant suspected it would be longer than that, but it was obvious that Emily wanted to continue. If they had had any chance of reaching Maillochauds today, Grant knew that Emily would have insisted on going there. "It'll be an hour if Hortense doesn't break down," he cautioned.

"She won't," Emily said fiercely. "She'd better not!"

Though the car did not break down, Grant saw the strain that each mile etched on Emily's face. She was silent for most of the drive, and even when they had arrived and were eating supper at the small inn, she was unusually quiet. A dozen times, Grant started to ask Emily what was wrong, and a dozen times he bit back his words. He wouldn't pry, not when she had asked him not to.

But when they had retired to their rooms and he could hear the sound of her pacing through the thin walls, Grant could bear it no longer.

He knocked on Emily's door. "Let me in."

"I need to be alone."

Grant couldn't let her be alone any longer, for he knew how darkness magnified fears. "You're wrong," he told her. "Either you come out, or I'm coming in."

For a long moment, there was silence, and Grant feared that she would not answer him. Then he heard footsteps, and the door opened. Silently, he took Emily's arm and led her to the small courtyard behind the inn. He had seen a grape arbor with a bench beneath it. It was there that Grant directed Emily.

"Now tell me what's wrong," he said when Emily was

seated. The fact that she had come without protest was another measure of her distress. The old Emily would have at least asked where he was taking her. "I won't believe you if you tell me that it's nothing," he continued.

Grant took the seat next to Emily and turned so that he could watch her face. Though shadowed, he could see her expression. Her lips were pursed as if she were fighting pain, but at least the tears had stopped.

"It's not nothing." Emily's voice quavered, making Grant realize how close to the surface tears remained. "I'm afraid. I'm afraid of what I'll find in Maillochauds."

Grant wasn't surprised. There was nothing else that would have caused her so much anguish. "Do you want to talk about it?"

At first Emily did not reply. She tipped her head to one side, as if she were listening to the hoot of a barn owl and the soft rustling of nocturnal animals. At last she began to speak, her words halting at first. Then as she described the darkness she had experienced and her fear, the words began to pour forth like water over a dam. "I keep telling myself that it was nothing more than a cloud and that my imagination has run wild, but no matter how hard I try, I can't forget the darkness. I don't want to believe in omens, Grant, but I can't stop myself." Emily took a deep breath. "I can't lose Theo. I can't!"

Grant, who knew all too well how it felt to lose a loved one, ached as he shared her pain. He had encouraged her to talk. One of the doctors Grant had interviewed had told him that when soldiers experienced trauma, talking about it was as important as lancing a festering wound. Both released the poison and started the healing process.

Grant had done that, but there had to be something more he could do to help Emily. Though the lines that bracketed her mouth had disappeared, she still appeared vulnerable and alone. But she wasn't alone. Somehow Grant had to convince her of that.

He rose and drew Emily to her feet. Though she looked startled, she stood. Slowly, Grant wrapped his arms around Emily and pulled her close. She was a tall woman, but she fit in his embrace as if she'd been made for it.

The evening was cool and damp, filled with the scents of wet leaves and freshly turned earth. For others, it was an ordinary night, but for Emily nothing would be ordinary again until they had reached Maillochauds and she knew the truth about her brother.

"I wish I could guarantee that when we find Theo, nothing will be wrong," Grant said, "but I can't. Life doesn't come with guarantees."

Emily shivered, then moved closer to him. Grant wasn't certain whether she found comfort or simply warmth by being next to him. It didn't matter. He tightened the circle of his arms, wishing there were something more he could do to help her.

"I'm so afraid." Grant heard the catch in Emily's voice. "I can't bear the thought of losing Theo." She tilted her head and looked up at Grant, her eyes filled with anguish. "I know it's selfish of me. So many others have lost loved ones. Why should I think I'm special and don't need to make the same sacrifice?"

"You are special, Emily." Grant brought his hand up and stroked her cheek. "Don't ever doubt that."

As she shook her head, a lock of hair escaped from her chignon and curled around Grant's finger. It was soft and silky, almost as soft as her cheek. "I don't feel special," Emily said. "I feel frightened."

That was a feeling Grant knew all too well. "We all have fears. What's important is to fight them."

Emily's eyes widened. For the first time, he saw a hint of something other than pain reflected in them. Emily was curious. Her trembling had subsided. Grant wasn't sure whether it was the fact that he was holding her or the words he was saying, but he didn't care. The result was all that mattered.

"I don't know how to fight fear," she said. "I've always been able to chase unhappiness away by looking for a silver lining, but this is different. I can't find a single one. I've tried all day, and all I've done is fail. My fears are too strong."

Grant wasn't going to admit that he didn't always emerge victorious in his battle with fear. That was one thing Emily didn't need to know. "When I'm frightened," he said, "I whistle in the dark."

Emily raised an eyebrow. "You whistle in the dark?"

He nodded. "That's my trick. You could say it's like your quest for a silver lining. I don't know why, but it works."

Grant saw a glimmer of amusement in Emily's eyes. Amusement was even better than curiosity. "You sound like my sister Carolyn." He hadn't been mistaken. Emily found his suggestion humorous. Her voice was lighter than before, close to a chuckle. "Carolyn dances in the rain."

That was something Grant had never done. In truth, he had done very little dancing in his life, either in the rain or out of it. Still, he found the idea intriguing. "I'd like to meet Carolyn," he said. "I think I'd like her."

Emily nodded. "Everyone likes Carolyn."

That's right. Carolyn was the sister that Emily claimed had attracted all the young men in Texas. "Ah, yes, the beautiful Carolyn Wentworth." Though Grant had little interest in discussing Emily's sister, he was grateful that she was no longer talking about Theo. Emily had needed a distraction, and if her sister provided that, Grant was happy. He would keep talking about Carolyn. "If I were a betting man, I'd wager you a tidy sum that you're far more beautiful than she." Though Emily insisted otherwise, Grant could not imagine that any woman could be more beautiful than Emily herself.

"You'd lose the wager," she told him. This time there was no question about it. Emily was amused.

"I doubt it. Now, are you going to try whistling?"

"Indeed I am." And she did.

An hour later when he was back in his room, Grant stood at the window, looking at the grape arbor and remembering. It had felt so good, holding Emily in his arms. Though he had meant only to comfort her, holding her close had brought him comfort. When Emily had been in his arms, Grant had felt as if an empty place deep inside him was filled. The strangest part was that he hadn't realized he had had an empty place until tonight. Somehow Emily had filled it. That was good, almost as good as being able to make her laugh. Others might not consider it a great feat, but when Emily had tried to whistle and had laughed at her first tentative attempts, Grant had felt as if he had accomplished something truly important.

He clenched his fists. It was foolish of him. He knew that. He shouldn't let himself care so much about Emily. Caring was dangerous, and Grant was a man who avoided danger when he could. He had learned his lessons at an early age; he knew the pain that caring brought. But when he had heard Emily cry out, he couldn't help himself. He had wanted—no, he had *needed*—to help her.

A cloud scudded across the moon, obscuring it for a few seconds. As it did, Grant felt as if a cloud had settled over him, obscuring his common sense. He shouldn't care about Emily, and yet he did. Somehow, though it was the last thing he had intended, Grant had let himself care about another human being. Not just another, but one very special woman. What he didn't know was how it had happened. In the past, he had always been able to maintain a safe distance from others. Oh, he was friendly with them, but he had never gone beyond casual friendship. This was different. What he felt for Emily was much more than casual friendship. He cared. Deeply.

Why? What was different this time?

Grant closed his eyes for a second and tried to reason. In the distance, he heard the sound of an airplane. That was it. It must be the war. He knew from the men he had interviewed that being part of a war heightened senses. Men in the trenches told him they felt more deeply about many things than they had at home. Grant nodded, relieved. That was why he felt about Emily the way he did.

It was the war. That was all.

Emily wakened with a smile on her face. The sun was shining, but as she poured water into a basin and prepared to wash her face, she knew that wasn't the reason for her smile. She pursed her lips and began to whistle. Grant was right. Though it made no logical sense, whistling didn't sound the same at dawn as it did in the dark. Emily hadn't been very good at whistling last night, but it hadn't seemed to matter then. This morning her whistling sounded as tuneless as her singing, and yet it still managed to comfort her. Emily smiled again and reached for the sliver of soap.

It was surprising how different she felt today. Yesterday, she had been convinced that she would not reach Theo in time, and that had terrified her. Though she had tried to deny it by pretending that nothing was wrong, her fears had been so strong that they had almost paralyzed her. Today her worries seemed fewer. Emily whistled a few notes. The reason wasn't hard to find. It was Grant.

She smiled as she slid her arms into her dress and buttoned the cuffs. It had felt so wonderful, being in Grant's arms. Emily had never dreamed that anything could feel so good. For a few minutes, she had felt safe and protected and something else, something she wasn't sure she could describe. Somehow, even without saying a word, Grant had comforted her. And when he had spoken . . . Emily smiled again. She hadn't realized that anyone other than Theo could lighten her spirits the way Grant had. She hadn't thought anyone other than her brother could understand the way she felt. But Grant had.

Emily brushed her hair and coiled it into a chignon. Grant had helped her so much. Because of him, she felt ready to face today. Because of him, she had regained some of her optimism. Because of him, she had a weapon against fear.

Grant had told her she was special. Emily didn't believe that, but she knew without a single doubt that Grant himself was special. And that was part of the reason she wished she could help him. She knew he had secrets and that some of those secrets were fearful. Why else would he know that one way to keep fear at bay was to whistle in the dark? And why had he built walls to shield himself from others? Emily wished she knew.

Though she hadn't thought it possible, admitting her fears to Grant had helped lessen their power. He hadn't dismissed her fears as trivial. He hadn't told her she was foolish to fear. Instead, he had given her a way to fight those fears. Why wouldn't he let her help him in the same way? More than almost anything else, Emily wished Grant would confide in her. Even though he claimed that what had bothered him had been Theo, Emily sensed that was only part of the reason Grant had been worried. Though she didn't know why, he hadn't been willing to share his other concerns with her. Emily wanted to know Grant's deepest fears, and she wanted to help him vanquish them.

As she replaced her hairbrush in her clothing bag, Emily realized that she had never felt like this. She had never before felt truly connected to anyone other than Theo. It was understandable that she would feel that way about Theo. He was her twin. Grant was not. Why, then, did she feel the need to help him? Why, then, did she tingle when she thought of how it had felt, being held in the circle of his arms? There had to be a reason.

Emily folded the blanket and laid it on the foot of the bed. There had to be a reason why she felt so odd. As she lifted her bag, she heard the crinkle of Theo's last letter. The war. That must be the reason. She had never been in a war before. It was a terrible experience, one that she had heard made people value things differently. That must be why she felt so different. That must be the reason Grant seemed so important to her.

It was a fluke of the war. That was all.

Chapter Seven

They were traveling southeast now, making slow but steady progress toward Maillochauds. Today, fortunately, was another sunny day, and the road was nearly dry. Emily gave silent thanks that Hortense would be able to travel faster. Though Henry Ford was justifiably proud of his creation's ability to cross unplowed fields and vast expanses of mud, no one claimed that the car could do so at top speed.

Emily pressed the hand lever forward, urging the car to accelerate. It was strange, she reflected as she guided Hortense around a bend in the road, but she felt different than she had just a few days before. She had the same sense of urgency about reaching Maillochauds and finding Theo. Nothing could change that. But now she felt less frantic, less worried. While in the past she had feared that she would not find Theo, now Emily was confident that she would reach him. She was anxious to see her brother, but she was no longer paralyzed with fear. For the first time, she felt as if she was not alone.

Emily glanced at the man who sat beside her. This morning he was in one of his contemplative moods. Though his

91

eyes focused on the road in front of them, she suspected he was unaware of the hedges, the stone buildings or the occasional herds of cows. Instead, he seemed to be composing his next column. He would remain silent for 10 or 15 minutes, then would scribble a few words on a sheet of paper. That appeared to be enough. When they stopped for the day, Grant would turn those scribbles into a full column, and tomorrow morning he would telegraph it to his editor.

For a while at least, Grant was in his own world. Perhaps that should have made Emily feel that she was alone. It did not. Anyone who had observed them would have said that Emily had never been alone, for Grant had been with her from the beginning of the journey. That was true. He had been physically present. Now it was different. Ever since the night he had taught her to whistle in the dark, Emily felt that he was with her emotionally. Grant was now part of the search for Theo, not simply a passenger in the car. It was a subtle difference and yet an important one for Emily. She felt as if she had an ally, someone who understood the reason for her journey and who would do everything possible to help her succeed.

Emily hadn't realized how much lighter burdens felt when they were shared. That was what Grant had done. He had shared her fears, and in doing so, he had helped her vanquish the worst of them. The man was wonderful, no doubt about it. He was also an enigma. Though they had traveled together for days now, Emily still knew very little about him, other than the fact that he had once learned to whistle in the dark.

When he had scribbled a few words and returned his writing desk to the back seat, Emily turned to Grant. "What made you decide to become a writer?" She wasn't certain he would answer, for one of Grant's dominant characteristics was his reticence.

He looked at her for a long moment, as if trying to decide why she had asked the question. At last he said, "I'm not sure it was ever a conscious decision. Telling stories was something I'd always done. Eventually I realized that I could get paid for them."

"I imagine you read a lot as a child." Emily's sister Martha had. That was one of the reasons she had become a teacher, to encourage others to enjoy reading as much as she did.

"Every book I could find." Grant tapped his glasses, as if his poor eyesight were a result of excessive reading. "What about you?"

"I'm afraid I didn't read nearly as much as you did." Though Martha had claimed that reading was one of life's greatest pleasures, Emily had not been convinced. "For me, reading was something to do on a rainy day when Theo and my sisters were tired of playing Parcheesi. If the weather was nice, Theo and I were outside." Emily steered the car around a particularly deep rut. When Hortense was back in the middle of the road, Emily loosened her grip on the steering wheel. This was, she reflected, the first time she had spoken of Theo without pain gripping her heart. More of Grant's magic.

It was raining when she and Grant climbed into Hortense the next day. Though Emily had encountered many days of rain, never before had she seen such a torrential downpour.

"I guess our luck with the weather has ended," she said as she coaxed the motor to turn over. The deluge was so intense that she did not remove her sou'wester even when she was inside the car. Between the wind-driven rain and Hortense's open sides, there was little doubt that the front compartment would be wet today.

Grant finished drying his glasses on his handkerchief.

"The rain may be bad for us," he said frowning at the water that was rapidly filling the ruts in the road, "but the villagers will be happy."

"It'll be good for the crops." Emily knew farmers prayed for rain, especially at this time of the year when they'd just planted their crops.

As if he had read her thoughts, Grant shook his head. "People pray for rain because there's less bombing then. Flying is more dangerous in the rain, so it's rare to have air raids when the rain's this heavy."

Emily looked at the water that streamed off the car. "Then I'm thankful for the downpour."

She was not, however, thankful when Hortense sputtered to a stop. Nor was she thankful when she was unable to find anything wrong with the car's motor.

"I can't find the problem," she told Grant, not bothering to hide her frustration. "The light's so bad that I can hardly see anything." Though it was midday, the thick clouds made it appear to be dusk.

Grant shrugged as if to say that he wasn't concerned. "There's a building over there." He pointed to a small stone hut in the middle of a field. Though the surrounding buildings were missing roofs and walls, this one appeared to have survived intact. "I'd suggest we take shelter there until the storm is over. We can eat our meal inside."

Together, they raced across the field, spraying mud with each stride. Despite her coat and hat, Emily felt rivulets of rain slide down her back. As she blinked to clear her vision, she wondered whether Grant could see anything, for the rain was streaming down his spectacles.

When they reached the windowless building, Emily realized it was so small it had probably been used to store either grain or ice. That didn't matter. No matter how musty it smelled, it had to be drier than standing outside. The door was open a crack. Grant pushed the door open further, ges-

turing for Emily to enter. He was, she reflected, as cour-
teous as Monsieur Ferrand.

As she entered the tiny room, Emily heard a low growl-
ing. For a second she froze, not sure what kind of animal
was inside. Then she heard a tentative bark. The room was
only marginally darker than the outdoors, and Emily's eyes
adjusted quickly.

"Look, Grant. There's a dog." The animal stood in the
far corner, his hackles raised. Though he growled again, he
did not approach them.

"Are you certain that's a dog?" Grant did not bother to
hide his skepticism. He dried his glasses, then stared at the
animal again.

It was one of the most homely creatures Emily had ever
seen. This one had the misfortune to be part of a long-
haired species, and that long fur was matted and filthy. It
was also a dog whose ears were supposed to be long and
floppy. Unfortunately, only one fit that description. The
other had apparently been bitten off, for it was short and
ragged. Emily could not see its tail, but she suspected it
was as mangy as the rest of its body.

"Of course it's a dog." Emily glared at Grant. How could
he insult the poor creature? Couldn't he see that the dog
needed care? "Poor thing. Here, boy." Emily held out her
hand for the animal to sniff. He stared at her, then approached warily, his tail between his legs. "Good boy," she
said, keeping her voice low and friendly. The dog came
closer. When he gave her hand a swipe with his tongue,
she patted his head. He barked.

Emily's heart turned over when she saw how the animal's ribs protruded. How long had it been since the poor
creature had eaten? Emily reached into the cloth bag that
held their food and pulled out a loaf of bread. Breaking off
a chunk, she handed it to the dog. To her surprise, he did
not lunge for it but waited until she placed it on the floor

before he ate it. Someone had taught this animal manners and, despite his obvious hunger, he had not forgotten them.

"Now he'll be your friend for life," Grant said when Emily offered the dog a piece of sausage.

Why was the man so cynical? "He came to me before he knew I had any food."

Grant considered her words for a second. "That's true," he admitted. "Perhaps we have a case of beauty and the beast. The beast couldn't resist you."

Emily flushed at the thought that Grant considered her a beauty. He had said that before, and she still could not believe that it was true. Carolyn was the Wentworth beauty. Emily was the plain sister.

"I wonder who the poor thing belongs to," she said. She had taken off her coat and hat and was seated on the ground, preparing a simple lunch for her and Grant. Grant sat opposite her, his back against one wall, his long legs stretched out in front of him, regarding the dog with the same wary expression that the animal gave him. The similarity was almost enough to make Emily laugh.

"He probably doesn't belong to anyone anymore."

It was a somber thought. "Poor boy," Emily said, stroking the dog's back. He sat by her side now. "You need someone to take care of you." Though he knew that his food had come from the cloth bag, he made no move toward it.

"Emily, you can't save every animal you see. I know Pollyanna took in a cat and a dog, but she was only a character in a book."

Emily ignored Grant. "He needs someone to feed him and brush his fur and bathe him."

"I'd like to see you try that. Dogs hate baths."

"Really?" Emily considered the animal's filthy fur, then looked back at Grant. "I never had a dog. Theo and I always wanted one, but our parents said that four children were enough for them to raise." She handed Grant a piece of bread and some sausage. "You must have had a dog, though, if you know about bathing them."

Grant's smile was wry. "I found out the hard way. When I tried to bathe Augustus, he overturned the basin. Do you know how much of a mess five gallons of soapy water can make?"

Emily returned Grant's smile. "Augustus?" she asked. No one she knew had a dog named Augustus.

"I named him after the emperor of Rome.'

"Then I imagine he was a regal dog. Not like this poor animal."

Grant shook his head. "I'm afraid he was almost as homely as this one."

Emily was still trying to picture Grant with a pet. "How long did you have him?"

Grant's eyes darkened. He took another bite of food and chewed carefully before he replied. "Not long. I came back from school one day, and Augustus was gone. No one knew what had happened to him."

"Oh, Grant!" Tears sprang to Emily's eyes as she thought of how sad the young Grant must have been. "How awful for you!" She gave the mangy dog another pat, wondering if someone was missing him as much as Grant had obviously missed his pet.

"It was probably awful for Augustus." Grant rose and looked outside. "I think the rain is subsiding."

It was, Emily realized, no more than she should have expected. Grant obviously did not want to talk about his own losses. Instead, he did what he had done every time she ventured too far into his personal life: He changed the subject.

Grant's assessment of the weather proved accurate, and half an hour later, the rain had stopped. Grant and Emily walked across the field, the dog following closely. When

Grant climbed into the car and began to organize their belongings, Emily opened the hood and tried to diagnose Hortense's problem. The dog stood so close to her that she could feel the warmth of his breath on her hand when she lowered it to her side.

"Okay, boy, what do you think is wrong with this flivver?" she asked. As if he understood, the dog gave a short bark. Emily laughed. "Exactly. Hortense needs to learn to bark."

In truth, what Hortense needed was her magneto-to-coil wire tightened. Once Emily discovered that the wire was slightly loose, it took less than a minute to have the car running once again.

"Ready, Grant!" Between the breakdown and the rain, they had lost more than an hour, but now they were ready to continue their journey.

Grant cranked the motor. Emily started it. The dog whined. He stood next to Emily's door and stared at her, his expression clearly pleading.

"Oh, Grant. He wants to come with us? Do you mind?"

Grant looked at the woman who, even though her hair was plastered to her head and her clothing was mud-spattered, was the most beautiful woman he had ever met. Did he mind taking a mangy mutt with them? Indeed he did! But this was Emily, and he didn't want to hurt her by refusing outright.

"We're going into an even more dangerous area," he said, trying to appeal to her reason. "The dog could be hurt." That was true. What was also true was that Grant had absolutely no desire to accept responsibility for another living creature. That was the path to heartache.

"But he could starve if we leave him here." So much for logic. Emily had out-reasoned him. "Please, Grant," she said, her blue eyes imploring him to agree. "I promise I won't let him be a burden."

The dog would be a burden. Grant knew that. He also knew that Emily would be hurt if they left the mutt behind, and she'd worry about him if she didn't know what had happened to him. Not knowing was the worst part of losing someone or something, especially for a person with a vivid imagination. For months after Augustus had disappeared, Grant had imagined his pet in hundreds of different places, very few of which were pleasant. He had always thought Mrs. Schiller had taken Augustus to the pound, but he could never prove it, and so he had imagined and worried and, when the other boys were asleep, he cried.

Grant couldn't do that to Emily. He feared what the future was going to bring to this woman who had somehow managed to insinuate herself into his life and his dreams. Though Emily thought she was strong, she was vulnerable, as was anyone who cared too much. Though he had tried to encourage her, Grant was afraid of what she would find when she reached Maillochauds. He feared that the pain of discovering what had happened to Theo would be more than Emily could bear. Grant couldn't—he wouldn't—do anything to make it worse.

"All right."

Emily's smile was radiant, and suddenly the nuisance that the dog was sure to create didn't seem so bad.

"Thank you," she said, and to Grant's surprise, she leaned over and pressed a soft kiss on his cheek.

"Here, boy." When Emily opened the back door, the dog needed no further invitation. He jumped into the car, then placed his front feet on Emily's seat back and licked her neck.

When they'd gotten the dog settled, Emily turned to Grant. "I can't keep calling him 'dog' or 'boy.' He needs a name."

Grant looked at the creature in the back of the car. It

was without a doubt the ugliest animal he had ever seen. "What about 'Beast?' " he suggested.

Emily acted as if he had insulted her, when all he had been doing was trying to give the dog an appropriate name. "That's cruel, Grant. He deserves better than that."

Grant knew better than to name another animal after a Roman emperor. "Let's call him 'Beau.' "

" 'Bow?' Like bow tie?"

Grant shook his head. " 'Beau' as in French for handsome." Grant looked at the dog again and shrugged. "Who knows? Perhaps he'll live up to his name."

Chapter Eight

She hadn't meant anything by it. Grant grabbed his hat and headed toward the door. The last thing he wanted to do was to remain in this room until supper, remembering what had happened just a few hours earlier. He had been surprised when Emily had agreed to stop earlier than usual, but today, it appeared, was a day for surprises. And so they had stopped an hour before the normal suppertime, only to discover that the woman who ran this small hotel served her evening meal an hour later than most. Emily was in her room, doing whatever it was women did when they arrived in a new place, and Grant was left with two hours to fill.

He ought to be writing. Unfortunately, the only thoughts that whirled through his brain were decidedly inappropriate to share with his readers. Since he was unable to write, he ought to spend the time talking to others, perhaps finding a new subject for a column. Unfortunately, there were no other guests, and the innkeeper did not appear the sort who would appreciate companionship while she cooked. That left Grant with nothing to do but remember.

He touched his cheek, then frowned. It was foolish to assign any importance to Emily's gesture. It wasn't as if it were a real kiss. What she had given him had been no more than a friendly peck, something she would have bestowed on a brother.

Grant closed the door and stepped into the narrow hallway. The smells of cooked cabbage and onion assailed him, and he wrinkled his nose, as much at the realization that Emily regarded him the same way she did Theo as at the odors that rose from the kitchen. It was odd. All his life he had wished he had a brother or sister. Now that a woman treated him like a sibling, he was angry. Truly, this war was turning everything upside down.

Grant took another step, then stopped as he nearly tripped over the mangy mutt who lay in front of Emily's door, obviously waiting for his newfound savior to come out.

"C'mon, Beau," Grant said. Maybe if he took the dog for a walk, he would stop thinking about things that were best forgotten. Like the kiss. There was absolutely, positively, categorically no reason to assign any special significance to it. There was certainly no reason to remember how soft Emily's lips had felt and how he wished she had missed his cheek and touched something else—his lips, for example.

When Beau realized they were going outside, he raced down the stairs, then stood at the foot, staring up at Grant, as if to ask why he was so slow.

"Sorry, buddy," Grant said. "Some of us have only two legs."

Unbidden, Grant remembered how graceful Emily's ankles were. Even the old-fashioned high-button shoes that she sometimes wore could not hide their shapeliness. What was wrong with him? He ought to know better to entertain such thoughts of Emily. Thinking about how beautiful she was was just as foolish as remembering how sweet her kiss had felt. After all, once they reached Maillochauds and she was reunited with her brother, Emily would have no reason to see Grant again.

He opened the door and let Beau outside. The dog bounded down the front stairs, his enthusiasm in sharp contrast to Grant's glum thoughts. Of course he and Emily would part ways in Maillochauds. That was what he wanted, what he had always wanted. Grant had known from the beginning that his friendship—surely that was all it was—with Emily would end. Friendships always did. Anyone he cared about left. That was why he had long ago determined that he would not let anyone get close enough that their leaving would hurt. That was why he had kept his relationships with others superficial. He had always been successful. Until Emily. When she left . . . Grant refused to think about the emptiness that Emily's leaving would cause.

"C'mon, Beau," he called. "You're going to learn how to chase a stick."

Where was Beau? Emily looked down the narrow corridor, expecting to see the dog. When she had refused to let him into her room—it was crowded enough without a large dog whose exuberant tail-wagging would knock objects onto the floor—he had reluctantly laid his head on his paws and camped in front of her door. Now he was gone. Emily started to knock on the door next to hers, then stopped. Even though there was a remote possibility that Beau might be there, she needed more time before she saw Grant again.

She shouldn't have done it. There was no question about that. Emily should not have kissed Grant. It wasn't simply that her sisters would have been scandalized by the fact that she'd kissed a man. That didn't matter. What mattered was the way that kiss had made her feel. Emily laid her fingers on her lips, then frowned. She needed to put that moment of madness behind her.

Beau. She would think about Beau. The poor dog needed her, whereas Grant . . . *Stop it!* Emily admonished herself. She descended the stairs, forcing herself to think only about where the dog might have gone. She stopped at the kitchen door and asked the proprietor of the small inn two questions.

"Outside, *mademoiselle,*" the woman answered the first, gesturing toward the front door. "*Certainement,*" she agreed when she heard the second.

The evening was cool and, even though a light mist still hung in the air, the rain had stopped. Emily smiled when she saw Beau racing in circles, apparently chasing his tail. Though Emily had never had a dog, she had watched others entertain themselves in a similar fashion. This must be the way solitary dogs played. Beau pricked his ears and began to run toward a stand of trees. A second later, he returned, a stick clenched in his mouth.

"Good boy!"

Beau was not alone. Grant was playing catch with him. Emily took a deep breath and exhaled slowly in a vain attempt to return her heartbeat to normal. Despite her best efforts, it raced at the sight of the man who was never far from her thoughts. Even in the gathering dusk, Emily could see that Grant looked different. His shoulders seemed relaxed, and his face appeared almost carefree. Though he was not smiling, there was something lighthearted about his whole demeanor. For this moment at least, Grant appeared to be a man whose primary mission in life was ensuring that one oversized dog learned to fetch a stick.

"Fetch, Beau, fetch!" Grant hurled the stick into the distance, his eyes focused on the dog.

Emily's eyes remained focused on Grant. Though she told herself to think about Beau or the threat of rain or even the cabbage soup that would be their supper, Emily's thoughts returned to Grant, remembering how it had felt to kiss him. While her cheeks were soft, his were firm. While hers were smooth, his were a little prickly from the stubble of his beard. Unbidden, Emily's fingers touched her lips, recalling the tingling sensation that the touch of her lips on Grant's cheek had wrought. Who would have thought that such a casual gesture, a mere touching of lips to cheek, would have sent shivers of delight throughout her body? She had meant the kiss as nothing more than a gesture of thanks, but it had been more, much more.

This was ridiculous! Emily took a step closer to Grant and Beau. She shouldn't care about how good it had felt to touch Grant. It had been a matter of seconds. It wasn't as if it would ever happen again. It wasn't as if they had a future. When they reached Maillochauds, her path and Grant's would diverge, and she would never see him again. Those were the terms of their agreement. They would remain together as long as it took to get Emily to Maillochauds. Once she and Theo were reunited, Grant would be free to continue on his way, unencumbered by a woman who had the bad habit of picking up stray animals.

That was the way it had to be. Grant was not a man who made long-term commitments, and Emily was not a woman to inspire them. Emily was Theo's sister, the boys' pal, and—today—Beau's rescuer.

"Evening, boys!"

Grant turned and grinned at her. "Are you calling us?" His smile made him look younger and more relaxed than she had ever seen him. Was this what Grant had looked like as a boy when he had had Augustus? If so, Emily was doubly glad they had found Beau. It appeared the dog wasn't the only one who was benefiting from being adopted.

"I certainly am calling you," Emily replied. "The water should be ready."

"What water?"

Though Emily knew it was impossible, Beau gave her a look that seemed to say he understood the word and disapproved. Or perhaps it was only that he recognized the skeptical tone of Grant's voice. Deciding to play along, Emily whispered, "The water for Beau's bath."

"I thought I explained to you the lack of affinity dogs have for baths." As Grant ruffled the fur at Beau's neck, the dog looked up, his expression clearly adoring. Grant might have accused her of buying the dog's affection by feeding him, but there was no doubt that Beau had been won over by a game of fetch and some simple affection. "You wouldn't do that to Beau, would you?" Grant asked.

Emily was not dissuaded. "Whether or not he likes it, Beau needs a bath—desperately." That was one of the reasons she had forbidden him entry to her room. Weeks of living in the wild had left Beau with a distinctly unpleasant smell.

Grant shrugged. "I can't argue with that." His voice was filled with sympathy as he looked down at Beau. "C'mon, boy. You're not going to like this, but the results will be worth it." He led the dog into the hotel's courtyard where the proprietor had placed a large tub of water and two smaller ones.

Afterwards, Emily admitted that the scene had been almost comic. As soon as he had seen the washtub, Beau had started to run in the opposite direction. Fortunately, Grant had anticipated the dog's reaction and quickly collared him. "Sorry, boy," he said as he lifted the animal and plopped him into the warm water. "This is for your own good."

Beau had snorted at his hero-turned-villain and looked at Emily with pleading eyes. But she had shaken her head and reached for the soap. While Grant held the dog, Emily rubbed soap into his fur, trying to ignore Beau's whimpering and the way he growled when she inadvertently got soap in his eyes.

"Let me help." Grant reached for the basin of rinse water that Emily was preparing to pour over Beau.

She hadn't meant for it to happen. She had been so careful to keep her hands away from his. But when she handed him the water, their fingers touched. It was nothing, nothing at all, and yet the tingles that Grant's touch sent racing up her arm could not be ignored. This was like the kiss that she had given him, a simple act which had repercussions that were far from simple. Emily felt color rush to her face as she remembered how it had felt to touch Grant's cheek. That felt almost as wonderful as this. It was foolish to put such stock in casual touches. What she needed to do was make certain that they were not repeated.

When at last Beau was clean, Grant lifted him out of the tub and placed him on the ground. For a second the dog stood motionless. With his sopping wet fur, he appeared almost as bedraggled as when Emily had first seen him, and she felt a twinge of regret for having made him so miserable. Then all regret evaporated as Beau glared at Grant and Emily and began to shake himself. Emily hadn't realized that an animal could move so quickly, or so violently, or that one dog's fur could contain so much water. Drops flew in all directions, spraying both Emily and Grant.

"Do you suppose that was his revenge?" Emily couldn't help laughing as she tried to shake the water from her skirt.

Though Grant tried to frown at Beau, the corners of his mouth refused to turn down, and soon both he and Emily were laughing while Beau continued to shake. Emily's laugh stopped abruptly as Grant reached forward and touched the bridge of her nose, his finger stroking its length. She knew that her eyes widened in surprise and that a blush stained her cheeks. Why was Grant touching her?

When their fingers had met before, it had been accidental. This was deliberate. Why? Even more importantly, why did his lightest touch make her shiver with pleasure? It wasn't as if this were a caress, and yet Emily was reacting as if it were.

"Soap." Grant held out his finger, showing Emily what he'd brushed off her nose. "I didn't think you wanted to wear it to dinner. Although I might be mistaken, I don't believe soap on the nose is the latest Parisian fashion."

Emily shook herself mentally. Grant's words confirmed what she knew instinctively. His touch had not been personal. It was a casual gesture, the kind of thing he would have done for anyone. It was only she who was overreacting, she whose whole face had warmed simply because he'd touched one part of it. Silly, silly Emily.

"My sister Carolyn would tell you that the fashion is to wear a clothespin on your nose," Emily said, trying desperately to think of something, anything other than how good it had felt to have Grant touch her.

"Is she the same sister who dances in the rain?"

Emily nodded. This was good. They would talk about Carolyn. That was much better than thinking about Grant and his touch. "No, Beau, you can't run in the mud." The dog was looking longingly at the puddle in the middle of the yard. "I'm going to brush your fur."

There was no doubt that Beau needed his fur groomed. Now that it was clean, Emily had resolved to try to brush out the tangles. Beau had other ideas, though. He appeared to believe that the brush was an instrument of torture, second only to the tub of water. As soon as Emily reached for him, he darted away, leaving Grant to chase him.

"I'll hold him." Grant placed the dog on top of the bench and kept his arm around Beau's neck.

The technique worked. Beau remained upright and, except for a few whimpers, silent. Though it was tedious work, Emily was able to coax the tangles from his fur. The problem wasn't Beau. It wasn't his fur. It was the fact that, try though she might, Emily could not avoid touching Grant. And each time she did, it was like the first time. Each time she felt a shock that reminded her of the day she had crossed two wires on the Model T. The only difference was, that shock had been painful. This one was not. It most definitely was not painful.

When she finished grooming Beau, Emily stood back and admired him. "You really are handsome."

Grant grinned. "Why, thank you."

Emily couldn't help it. She laughed. "I was talking to Beau."

Grant feigned indignation. "That dog gets more attention than I do."

"He needed it."

"I won't argue that point. It's simply that I never thought I'd be jealous of a dog."

He was joking, of course. After all, Emily was not the kind of woman who inspired jealousy in any man. But maybe someday there would be someone who would look at her the same way Monsieur Ferrand looked at his wife. Maybe someday there would be a man who loved her.

That night, Emily dreamed that she was back in Canela. It was evening, and she had come out of her parents' home. She moved slowly across the front porch, walking as if she were not sure where she was going. And then she saw him. He smiled as if he were waiting for her. He smiled as if she were the most beautiful woman he had ever seen. As she took another step forward, he rose from the porch swing, and this time his smile was one of invitation. She needed no further encouragement. Though she had been moving slowly, now she had a purpose.

Her pace quickened. When she reached him, he helped her into the swing, settling himself at her side. Then, as easily as if he had done it a hundred times, he slid his arm around her shoulders and drew her close to him. He smiled again, and as he did, Grant lowered his lips to hers.

Emily awoke with a start. Why had she dreamed of Grant? This was worse than the ridiculous way she blushed and her heart pounded whenever she and Grant touched. Now she was dreaming that he was regarding her the way Monsieur Ferrand did his wife. That wasn't just ridiculous; it was impossible. Emily knew that Grant kept barriers between himself and others. He wasn't a man who would let himself fall in love, and even if he were, Emily wasn't the woman he would love.

Then why, oh why, had she dreamed of him? There had to be a logical reason. Perhaps it was because Emily had been thinking of love, and Grant was the only single man she had seen in days. That must be it. There couldn't be any other reason. Still, Emily wished Martha or Carolyn were nearby. More than any time she could remember, she wished her sisters were close enough for her to talk to them, to ask why—no matter how hard she tried not to—she kept thinking of Grant.

Fortunately, the sun was shining the next day. Though Beau appeared tempted to roll in one of the remaining mud puddles, Grant had made him a rope leash and kept him close to his side until they reached the car. Once there, Beau had leaped into the back seat and sat there, his proud posture reminding Emily of a painting she had once seen of a duke riding in his carriage. Never before had he sat so tall with his head tipped at an almost regal angle. Perhaps he was proud now that he was clean. Perhaps Grant had been right and Beau was going to live up to his name.

For the first hour, everything went well. Then they reached the bridge. Or, rather, what had once been a bridge. The stone footings remained, but the bridge itself was gone, washed away by the stream that still overflowed its banks.

"I don't have to ask, do I? Hortense isn't going to ford that stream." As Emily shook her head, Grant pulled out the map and handed it to her. To Emily's dismay, there appeared no easy detour. They would have to return to the town where they had spent the night and take another road from there. That meant at least two hours lost.

"I don't like this," she told Grant. "I wish there were another way." Emily stood at the side of the car considering. "We passed a farmhouse a few minutes ago. Do you think it was occupied?" Emily had been steering around ruts and had paid little attention to anything other than the road surface.

Grant nodded. "I saw a plume of smoke."

"Then let's ask there. There may be an unmarked road."

Though the farmer's wife was clearly skeptical of Hortense, admitting it was the first automobile she had seen, she explained that there was a path to the next town. "It's a footpath," she cautioned. "Sometimes cows use it."

That was good enough for Emily.

Grant seemed to share the Frenchwoman's skepticism as they turned onto the narrow road. "Do you think Hortense will get through?"

Emily refused to think of the alternative. "She'd better." And she began to whistle. Perhaps that would keep her fears at bay.

"It's not dark," Grant pointed out.

To Emily's relief, Hortense continued along the rock-filled path. Perhaps whistling had benefits beyond chasing fears. Perhaps it brought good luck. Though the ride was decidedly uncomfortable, at least they were moving. "I discovered that your technique works even when the sun's shining." As Emily whistled again, Beau laid his feet on her seat back. "Down, Beau."

"He probably thought you were whistling for him."

Emily flashed a smile at Grant. "I think he's looking for food."

She herself was looking for ruts in the road and trying to avoid the largest of the rocks. Though Hortense was sturdily made, it would be tempting fate to drive over a boulder. When they reached the top of a small hill, Emily caught her breath.

"Oh, Grant, look!" She stopped the car and climbed out, astonished by the beauty of the scene before her. While they had passed towns that had been bombed and burned, by some miracle, the building on the next hill had escaped all damage. It stood there, its gray stone and crenellated towers unmarred by the war that surrounded them. Even the fields appeared to have suffered no damage. A flock of sheep grazed on the hillside outside the castle, their white wool providing a vivid contrast against the green grass. As castles went, this one was small—large enough for no more than a hundred people—but it was a gem.

"Isn't that the most beautiful house you've ever seen?" Grant stood at her side, and Emily turned toward him, smiling with delight. "It looks like something out of a fairy tale."

He raised one eyebrow and behind the spectacles his brown eyes mirrored his skepticism. "I thought you didn't read as a child."

Emily shrugged. "Everyone reads fairy tales." Her gaze returned to the castle. If she had been asked to describe the castle where Cinderella or Snow White lived, this would be it. The four corners were marked with perfectly symmetrical towers. It even boasted a moat. Though Emily suspected it would be beautiful in any weather, the deep blue sky with an occasional puffy white cloud gave the scene an air of almost otherworldly perfection. Looking at the castle and its pastoral setting, it was difficult to believe that a war raged only a few miles away.

"I wish I lived in a house like that." The words came out, seemingly of their own accord.

Grant chuckled. "That's what I like, a woman of simple tastes."

Emily took no offense at Grant's gentle ribbing. "I would prefer to say that I have dreams," she countered, then flushed when she remembered what she had dreamed the night before. To hide her confusion, she fixed her gaze on the castle on the hill. "Wouldn't it be wonderful to live there?" Emily blushed again as her mind conjured the image of herself standing by the moat, Beau at her side, as Grant returned to them.

Apparently oblivious to the traitorous direction her thoughts were taking, Grant shrugged. "I've never thought much about owning a house."

Emily stared at him. "Never?" She knew Grant lived a nomadic existence now, but surely after the war, he'd want to settle somewhere.

As if he had heard her unspoken question, Grant continued, "Since settling down has never been part of my plans, I haven't had a need for a house—no matter how simple."

There was something in Grant's tone that told Emily she had touched a sensitive nerve. She knew that he established barriers between himself and other people, even animals. Did he also shun the permanence of possessions? She shouldn't pursue it, and yet . . . "What kind of house did your parents have?"

As Emily had expected, Grant did not answer. Instead, she watched the flit of emotions on his face as he patted Beau's head. There was sorrow—she recognized that—and something else, something she could not identify. Could it possibly be hope?

Grant raised his gaze to meet hers and looked at her for a long moment. Then he said bluntly, "I don't know." It was not the answer she had expected, and Emily knew her face must have reflected her surprise. For another long moment, Grant said nothing. Emily tried to keep her expression impassive. Perhaps if she waited, he would tell her. He frowned and stared at the castle for a second. Then he turned back to Emily, his voice low as he said, "My parents died when I was only a few months old. I grew up in an orphanage."

The pain that engulfed Emily startled her with its intensity. "Oh, Grant!" He had told her that he had no siblings, but no parents? Emily could not imagine how alone he must have felt.

Grant shook his head, his voice fierce. "Save your pity for Beau. It wasn't that bad—not like something from one of Charles Dickens' books." Snapping his fingers, Grant called to the dog who had wandered a few feet away. "C'mon, Beau. Time to get back in the car."

As she started Hortense's engine again, Emily tried not to stare at the man seated next to her. How typical of Grant, changing the subject to something—anything—other than himself. He had done it every time she or anyone else had raised the topic of his childhood. And yet Emily could not forget that today had been different. For the first time, he had volunteered something about himself.

An orphanage. Emily steered the car around another boulder. That explained so much. No wonder Grant had refused to discuss his parents and had deflected questions about his childhood. Despite what he said, she did not believe that his had been a happy youth. It was understandable that he would not want to talk about it.

The question was, why had he spoken today? Why had he done what he had always refused to do? Why had he broken the silence? Emily's heart sang with pleasure as she considered the possibilities. There was only one that made any sense: Grant was starting to trust her. How wonderful that felt!

It was the best thing that had happened to her since she had arrived in France. Emily gripped the steering wheel. Why stop there? It was the best thing that had ever happened to her. Others might not consider it an accomplishment, but Emily did. Grant trusted her enough to confide in her. Even if only for a moment, he had lowered the barriers that he'd erected between himself and others. And he'd done it for Emily.

Nothing in her past had made her as happy as the knowledge that she had accomplished that. No matter what the future brought, she would always remember today . . . and Grant.

Chapter Nine

Grant stared into the distance. They had reached the end of the detour and were back on the main road. Though she had said nothing, Grant knew from the way Emily's shoulders relaxed that she was relieved to be off the cow path. He himself believed it no small miracle that Hortense had managed to travel the entire distance without so much as a hiccup. Perhaps that mechanical monster had psychic powers and knew when a breakdown would be fatal. Grant suspected Emily shared his amazement, for once they'd regained the main road, she had suggested they stop, ostensibly so Beau could stretch his legs. Grant hadn't been surprised when Emily's first action had been to open Hortense's hood and stare at the motor.

While Emily assessed their mode of transportation, Grant assessed the road before them. The countryside here was not as beautiful as it had been on the detour, but the road was wider and smoother. The absence of boulders in their way would not displease Emily. Grant was certain of that.

He glanced back at the car and the woman who bent over the engine, the woman who occupied far too many of his thoughts. Emily was unlike any woman he'd ever met.

In the past, Grant had found it easy to categorize people, but Emily was different. She defied categorizations. She was like a kaleidoscope, constantly changing. At one moment, she would be practical, insisting on checking every bolt in that infernal combustion engine. The next, she would prove to be idealistic, refusing to leave a wounded kitten by the side of the road or begging him to let a mangy mutt join them. And then, just as quickly, she would turn into a romantic, wanting to live in that house. House? It had been a castle, pure and simple.

Grant knew enough about French architecture to recognize that the chateau had been designed by the same man who had planned the final and most beautiful additions to the Loire Valley chateau Chenonceaux. Though smaller, Emily's castle had the same delicate lines, the same combination of fantasy and symmetry that made Chenonceaux so famous.

Grant looked at the woman whose eyes had filled with joy as she'd stared at the stone building. She hadn't had to say anything, but Grant knew that while she gazed at her castle of dreams, she was able to forget both the war and her fears for Theo. If that wasn't miraculous, Grant didn't know what was. No wonder Emily wanted to live there.

The odd part of it was, it wasn't only Emily who thought that castle was perfect for her. With no difficulty at all, Grant could picture her living there. Even odder was the feeling deep inside him that, were the war over, he would do everything in his power to give that castle on the hill to Emily.

Grant smiled, imagining Emily's pleasure when he told her that this would be her new home. She would smile that smile that turned her face from beautiful to positively radiant and made her eyes rival the sun for brilliance, and then he would see those dimples that he found so endearing. The imaginary scene changed. This time Emily was standing in front of the castle moat, Beau at her side, as Grant approached Emily's new home. Though he could not hear the words she murmured to Beau, Grant sensed a barely controlled impatience in both the woman and her dog. They were waiting for someone, and that someone was important. The longing that swept through Grant shocked him with its intensity. He wanted to be that someone!

In his reverie, though his impatience was as great as Emily's, he felt as if he were mired in quicksand, barely able to move. Then at last Emily saw him. She raised her hand in welcome, and her smile was joyful, as if he were the one she had been waiting for. "Welcome home."

Home? Grant shook his head as the word jolted him back to reality. Where had that thought come from? He looked at Emily. Yes, she was beautiful. Yes, he thought of her far more often than he should. And, yes, he wished she could have the castle on the hill. But that didn't mean that it would be his home. Most definitely not. Grant didn't want a home any more than he wanted a dog. Those were things meant for people like Emily, not Grant.

As she closed Hortense's hood, Emily turned toward Grant. "We're ready," she said with a smile. It was the same smile he had seen a hundred times. There was nothing wrong with it and certainly no reason to wish she were smiling the way he had imagined.

"Where's Beau?" Though she had smiled at Grant, her gaze moved quickly past him, looking for the dog.

Grant shrugged. "I thought he was with you."

"He was for a minute or two," Emily admitted. "Then he ran off. I thought you were playing together." Furrows appeared between Emily's eyes, visible proof that she was worried about Beau.

"I imagine he'll be back soon." Judging from the way he normally shadowed her steps, Beau was no more anxious to leave Emily than Grant was. If the dog had an imagination, which Grant sincerely doubted, he would probably picture himself with Emily at the castle on the hill. In all likelihood, though, Beau's fantasies were of chasing rabbits, not living in a castle, whereas Grant's . . .

It was simply proximity, of course. Grant knew it was common that when people spent as much time together as he and Emily had that they would start to believe that it would last forever. It wouldn't. He would feel differently once they reached Maillochauds. At that point, they would go their separate ways, starting the rest of their lives. Separate lives.

"We're ready to go." Emily looked at the sun, her eyes reflecting her desire to travel as many miles as possible each day. That was natural. She needed to reach her brother. It was only Grant who sometimes wished that their journey would never end. "I wonder where Beau is." Emily was visibly worried.

"Maybe if you started the motor, he'd hear it. I don't imagine he's gone far." Even if Beau were chasing rabbits, surely he would not let Emily and Grant leave without him.

Emily nodded, but before Grant could crank the starter, they heard the yelps. There was no mistaking them. The sounds were those of an animal in pain.

"It's Beau!" Emily jumped out of the car and began to run in the direction of the cries. The fields were muddy, and within a few yards, Emily's skirts were streaked with dirt. Grant was certain she neither noticed nor cared. If he knew Emily—and Grant believed he did—her only thoughts were for Beau and his injury.

Please, he prayed silently as he kept pace with Emily, *let it not be serious.* But the tenor of Beau's yelps told Grant that this was no minor scratch. The dog was in agony, his pain so severe that his cries reflected fear as well as injury. When they reached him, the reason was evident. Beau had fallen into a hunter's snare, perhaps as he chased the same rabbits that the hunter sought to catch. The cruel iron trap had crushed one of Beau's back legs, and the dog, struggling to free himself, had worsened the damage.

"Oh, Grant." He could hear the tears in Emily's voice as she knelt at the dog's side and began to pat his head. "We've got to get him out." Beau snarled and tried to bite Emily. "You'll be all right, Beau. We'll help you." Though tears dripped on the dog's fur, Emily's voice did not waver as she spoke to him.

Grant tried not to frown. "Let's see how bad it is," he said, wrenching the snare apart. Grant took a deep breath and tried not to reflect on the irony that death and destruction could occur on a beautiful sunny day in the middle of what appeared to be a perfectly peaceful field. He took another breath and examined Beau's leg. "Well, Beau, you certainly did some damage." As Grant moved the dog's leg, Beau yelped. Poor critter. He had quieted when Emily began to stroke him, but the leg had to hurt horribly.

"What can we do?" There was no ignoring the pleading in Emily's voice or the anguish that darkened those lovely blue eyes. With every fiber of his being, Grant wished he could tell her that Beau would be all right.

"I'm not a doctor, but . . ."

Emily cut him off. "Don't say it!" Her expression was fierce as she looked at the suffering animal. "Oh, Beau." As the tears that welled in her eyes tumbled down her cheeks, Emily began to whistle.

More than her tears, more even than the pleading in her voice, the whistling wrenched Grant's heart. He wished he were a doctor or a magician; he wished he could turn back time and keep Beau from running across the field. Most of all, he wished there were something he could do to keep Emily from suffering any more losses. For Grant feared that what they would find in Maillochauds would be so devastating that Beau's injury would pale in comparison.

"I know you're anxious to get to Maillochauds," Grant told Emily as he wrapped a clean rag around the dog's leg. "There's a field hospital near Aire. If you don't object to the delay, we could detour that way. There's a possibility that the doctors may be able to help Beau."

The expression on Emily's face made Grant feel as if he were one of history's legendary heroes, perhaps St. George after he'd slain the dragon. Not that what Grant had done was heroic. Far from it. But he wasn't going to quibble with the hope he saw in Emily's eyes and the way her lips had started to curve upwards. Nor was he going to quibble with the warmth that that smile had kindled deep inside Grant. He wasn't a hero. He was an ordinary man. And this ordinary man's mission was to protect Emily from pain. If that required sitting in the back of a Model T, holding an injured dog on his lap, so be it.

To Grant's infinite amazement, luck appeared to be on their side. When they reached the field hospital, they discovered that there had been a lull in the fighting, and as a result, the doctors had no queue of patients waiting for treatment. Equally promising, as they drove toward the half dozen tents that formed the field hospital, Grant spotted a physician he had met earlier in the war.

"Matt," he called to the man whose uniform was still immaculate despite hours in the operating theater. "I need you."

As Grant outlined his plan, Matt's eyebrows rose. He shook his head slowly. "Are you crazy? Why would you take on a burden like that?"

Grant's answer was simple. "I can't disappoint Emily."

The doctor's gaze returned to the Model T and its driver. Emily was lowering the tonneau cover to make it easier to get Beau out of the car. As she stretched her arms to unfasten the canvas, only a blind man would have missed seeing the lovely curves of her body. Matt was not a blind man. He stared at Emily for a long moment, then turned his attention to Grant. "So that's how it is." Though low, his words were tinged with amusement.

Grant clenched his fists to keep himself from planting one on the doctor's face. There was nothing amusing in the situation. Surely Matt could see that. "What do you mean?" Grant demanded.

Matt's amusement turned into a full-fledged grin. "Nothing. Nothing at all." He chuckled again, then sobered. "Bring in the dog."

An hour later, Grant emerged from the tent that served as an operating theater, carrying Beau in his arms. The dog lay motionless inside the blanket that Grant had wrapped around him. Though it was obvious that the nurses had tried to distract Emily, she jumped up from the table the instant she saw Grant.

"Don't blame yourself, Grant." Despite the tears that welled in her eyes, Emily's words were brave. "I know you did what you could, and I didn't want Beau to continue suffering. It's just . . ." Her voice cracked as the tears spilled down her cheeks. "Oh, Grant, there's too much dying in this awful war."

She had misunderstood. If he hadn't had his arms filled with an unconscious dog, Grant would have wrapped them around Emily to comfort her. As it was, the only comfort he could offer was words.

"He's not dead, Emily. The doctor had to anesthetize Beau when he set his leg." Gently Grant laid the dog on the back seat of the car and uncovered his face.

Emily stared at Beau. "He's alive?" Happiness vied with incredulity in Emily's voice. She touched the dog's face, and her own lit with joy as she felt Beau's breath. When she had satisfied herself that the dog was truly alive, Emily turned to Grant, her face radiant with happiness. "Oh, Grant! Thank you!" Though her eyes brimmed with tears,

Grant knew that these were tears of happiness, not sorrow. She blinked, trying to keep the tears from falling. "Thank you, Grant. You're wonderful."

She was mistaken. She was the one who was strong and brave and beautiful, and he wanted more than anything to show her that. "No, Emily. You're the wonderful one." And then before he could tell himself that it was wrong, he wrapped his arms around her and drew her close to him.

The rain had resumed, and to make it worse, Hortense had a flat tire. On another day, Emily might have been disgruntled or at least a little annoyed. But today nothing could dampen her spirits, for Beau was still alive. Despite that horrible accident, he was alive. He had wakened groggy, and had protested when Grant carried him into the bushes, but when Beau had seen the cast on his leg, his expression had been almost human: disbelief and then something that appeared to be anger, as if his body had betrayed him.

"Don't worry, Beau," Grant told the dog. "You'll soon be walking again."

He was wonderful. There was no doubt about it; Grant Randall was the most wonderful man she had ever met. Each day made her more convinced of that. Not only had he agreed to help her find Theo, but he'd done everything in his power to make this journey a pleasant one for her.

Grant had taught her to whistle in the dark. Then, almost as if he knew she doubted herself, he had started to confide in her. Had he known how much that trust meant to her? Perhaps he had, for Grant seemed to know almost everything. Like the right words to say to an over-worked field doctor to convince him to spend some of his precious time on a dog—an animal Grant hadn't even wanted to adopt. Like the way to hold a woman and make her feel cherished.

Emily's cheeks flamed as she remembered how wonder-

ful it had felt to be held in Grant's arms. Thank goodness
he was on the other side of the car and couldn't see her!
He would probably be embarrassed if he realized how she
had reacted to being in his arms. Emily knew that when
Grant had wrapped his arms around her, his only thought
had been to offer comfort. He would have done the same
thing to anyone—a small child, an elderly woman. It
wasn't as if he were *embracing* her. Far from it. He had
held her. That was different. Grant's gesture had been one
of simple human contact, the healing touch that her sister
Carolyn had told Emily worked wonders.

And it had, although perhaps in ways Grant had not intended. For Emily had felt comforted. Indeed, she had. But
within seconds, the comfort had changed to something else,
something warmer, more personal. This wasn't like being
held by her father, being comforted when she had skinned
her knee. When she had stood within the circle of Grant's
arms, Emily had been aware of Grant's warmth, the
strength of his arms, the firmness of his body. She had been
aware of him, not as Grant, her friend and traveling companion, but as Grant a man. Even stranger, Emily had been
aware of herself in new ways. For a fleeting moment she
had wished she were beautiful like Carolyn. She wished
her hair were bobbed and fashionable. She wished she were
clothed in a silk gown, not a serviceable white shirtwaist
and a gray skirt that was now caked with mud. Just as
quickly, her wishes had fled, replaced by the knowledge
that she wouldn't change anything.

It was wonderful—simply wonderful—being in Grant's
arms. Emily had cherished the memory of the night in the
garden when Grant had held her and taught her to whistle.
She had felt safe and comforted and something else that
night. Today had been much more. Today, though all he
had meant was to offer comfort, for a few minutes Grant
had made her feel as if she were the most important person

in the world. It was a moment out of time. She knew that. It had never happened before; it would probably never be repeated. But while it had lasted, it had been perfect.

Emily tightened the wheel, then stood up. Hortense was ready for another few miles. And she . . . she was as ready as she could be. They were only two or three days' journey from Maillochauds now. That particular thought filled Emily with more trepidation than she had believed possible. She would find Theo there. She had to. And yet, lurking at the back of her consciousness, ready to pounce when she least expected it, was the fear that Theo was not there, that she had imagined he was calling to her and that, even if he had been calling to her, he had not been saying Maillochauds.

Emily climbed into the car, smiling when she saw that Grant was leaning over the seat, talking to Beau. There was nothing she could do to allay her fears for Theo other than to whistle in the dark and concentrate on happier thoughts, like the way Grant appeared to be getting attached to the dog. The man didn't want to form an attachment to Beau, or to any animal, for that matter. He had made that clear from the beginning. That was why Emily was so amused— and so very pleased—by the care Grant took to ensure that the dog rested comfortably. He would deny it, but she had seen him sneak bits of his meat to Beau. And, though he had told her that cheese was bad for canine digestive systems, she had caught him breaking off a bit of particularly tasty Gorgonzola and feeding it to the dog.

Emily smiled, remembering Grant's chagrin when she had given the cheese a pointed glance. He'd been like a small child, caught pilfering from the cookie tin. Grant had held up his hands in a gesture of surrender, and while they'd both been laughing, Beau had extended a front paw to knock the plate of cheese onto the ground. Emily and

Grant had redoubled their laughter at the dog's cunning. For a few moments, the war had been forgotten.

That had been good. What had been better—much better—was the way Emily had felt when she'd been held in Grant's arms. That was the memory she would recall whenever her fears for Theo grew too strong. That was the memory she would cherish, not only now but for the rest of her life.

Chapter Ten

It was raining again. Emily gripped the steering wheel. When the road was this wet, the mud was almost as slippery as snow. Rain was never a surprise. In fact, her sister Carolyn had warned her that it was the typical weather in this part of France. However, rain as heavy as this was not normal. Emily peered through the windshield, trying to see the road despite the downpour, trying to find something positive about the day. She could start with the fact that Grant was in one of his contemplative moods. He had told her that never before had he had so much inspiration for his columns. That relieved Emily of the fear that her journey was hurting Grant professionally.

Next in the line of positives was the fact that Hortense had had no breakdowns in the past two days. That was close to the record. Then there was the fact that the rain was warm. Though there was no way to avoid getting drenched whenever they left the car, at least she and Grant were not risking illness. That was good.

So, too, was the fact that Beau's leg appeared to be healing properly. Emily slowed the car more than usual as she approached a bend in the road. Although the Model T's durability was renowned, and it was theoretically possible to upright the car and continue driving even after it toppled onto its side, Emily had no desire to prove that particular theory, especially with Beau in the back seat.

The doctor had warned Grant that the dog should not attempt to walk for a few days, and Grant had taken him seriously, never complaining that he had to carry Beau in and out of the car, and the small inns where they had been staying. Beau, too, had been amazingly cooperative. Though Emily had expected the active dog to protest his unexpected immobility, he seemed to understand what had happened. After the first time that he had chewed on his cast and been reprimanded by Grant, the dog had never again touched his leg.

The only problem occurred each night, when Beau whimpered and tried to follow Emily into her room. Since Grant had primary care of Beau during the day while she was driving, Emily had suggested that she take responsibility for him at night. Grant had proven surprisingly resistant to that idea, asking Emily what she would do if the dog needed to go outside during the night. Nothing she had said had convinced Grant that she was capable of carrying the dog down a flight of stairs. Grant was, Emily reflected, like a medieval knight. It appeared that he believed she was the lady to whom he'd pledged his fealty, and that one of his responsibilities was caring for her dog.

Grant was scribbling now. Emily added that to her list of things for which she was grateful. Scribbling meant that soon she'd be able to talk to Grant. She frowned as she looked at the horizon. Though the sun had not emerged from the dense rain clouds all day, the darkening told her that the hour was late. She had been afraid of that. They had had to make another detour because of a washed out bridge. Unlike their first detour, which had led them past the fairytale castle, this one had ended in a second stream that they were unable to ford. To Emily's dismay, there had been no alternative but to turn around and retrace their path. The result was a loss of at least three hours. Now she worried about how much longer they would be able to drive.

As if he sensed her thoughts, Grant pulled out his watch. "I don't think we'll get to Norrent before dark," he said, referring to the town they'd selected as today's stopping point. From the beginning, they had both agreed that they would not drive after dark, because the dangers were too great. Not only might they drive off the road or hit a boulder, but Hortense's lights would also make them a target for enemy bombers. They were so close to the front line now that raids were a serious concern.

Emily nodded. This was what she had feared. "There are no towns between here and Norrent." She had memorized the map, as she did each morning.

"If it weren't raining and if we weren't so close to the trenches, I'd say we could camp outside." Grant frowned at the windshield. "This is obviously neither the optimum weather nor location for that."

Beau, who'd been sleeping on the back seat, began to whimper.

"I think he's agreeing with you." Emily tried to make light of their predicament, though she was more concerned about the road conditions than she wanted to admit to Grant. The mud was so slippery that she feared they should stop for the day rather than risk sliding off the road. "Do you have any suggestions?"

Grant pushed his spectacles back on his nose, then touched the bump. It was, Emily knew, a sign that he was thinking. "Let's stop at the next farm we pass. If they don't have room for us, they may let us stay in the barn."

"At least we'd be dry." Though it would be unpleasant, Emily was confident she could spend a night outside, and she knew from Grant's stories that he'd spent many a night in the elements. The problem was Beau. The doctor had told Grant it was important to keep his leg dry if it was going to heal properly. That was why Grant covered Beau with a blanket when it rained. Even though the doors made Hortense's back seat drier than the driver's compartment, the car was far from watertight.

It was half an hour later when Emily drove down the narrow lane that led to a farmhouse. The stone building was more than twice as large as the Ferrands' had been, and to Emily's relief, there were no obvious signs of damage. Although the enemy had destroyed many of the homes along this road, this one was still standing and appeared to be occupied, for a plume of smoke rose from the chimney. Perhaps their luck was improving.

Obviously attracted by the unexpected sound of Hortense's motor, a gray-haired woman pulled aside a curtain and peered at them.

"I'll talk to her." Matching his actions to his words, Grant jumped down from the car and sprinted to the door. Only seconds later, the woman opened the door. Emily watched Grant gesturing and wondered what he was saying to persuade the woman.

"Our luck is holding," Grant told Emily when he returned to the car. "Madame Vigny says she has plenty of room for us. You, too, Beau." He lifted the dog into his arms. "She was about to eat supper and has invited us to join her."

Emily smiled. Though she and Grant had purchased food earlier in the day, there was no doubt that it would be more pleasant to eat a warm meal. And Grant, she suspected, was already thinking of ways to turn this experience into a column.

"*Merci, madame,*" Emily said as she greeted the Frenchwoman. "*Vous êtes très gentille.*" The truth was, Mme. Vigny had been far more than kind. Though hospitality was universal, Emily wasn't certain she would have been as welcoming to strangers, had she been in the middle of a war. "I'm Emily Wentworth, and this is . . ."

"Your husband," Mme. Vigny completed Emily's sentence as she hung her sou'wester on one of the hooks that lined the front hallway. "I understand. I may be a widow, but I still remember when I was a new bride like you."

Husband? Bride? What was the woman thinking? Emily was so astonished by Mme. Vigny's assumptions that she barely saw the whitewashed walls and polished floor as their hostess led them to the kitchen.

"But, madame, we're not married." What an absurd thought! It was surely the absurdity that made Emily's heart pound. It couldn't be anything else.

"No, we're not." Grant added his assurances to Emily's.

The Frenchwoman shrugged and quickly added two place settings to the table. "Married, about-to-be-married. It makes no difference. You can't hide the way you feel about each other. Love like yours shines even brighter than . . ." She looked around the kitchen, then pointed at her gleaming copper pans. "Even brighter than my skillet."

The skillet was bright. Grant and Emily's love was . . . nonexistent. "But, madame . . ." Somehow Emily had to make her understand.

The woman patted Emily's hand, then ladled soup into three bowls. "My dear, when it comes to love, you should never argue with a Frenchwoman." Mme. Vigny took her place at the head of the table, barely pausing to take a breath. "After all, who do you think invented romance? Why, it was our own Queen Eleanor of Aquitaine's daughter who started the courts of love during the Middle Ages."

Emily decided not to point out that Eleanor of Aquitaine was as much English as she was French. That would resolve nothing, nor would it convince Mme. Vigny that Emily and Grant were traveling companions, nothing more.

"But, madame . . ."

"This soup is delicious, madame." Grant made a show of savoring the vegetable and cheese broth. "It was truly masterful, the way you added a pinch of nutmeg."

Mme. Vigny nodded regally, accepting the compliment. "Always with cheese, monsieur. Always."

What was masterful was Grant. The man was definitely a master at changing subjects. Emily knew that he'd honed his skill over years of deflecting questions about himself, but she wasn't arguing with the fact that she was now the beneficiary of that talent. She took another spoonful of soup and tried to relax. Other than the shutters that were tightly closed, lest the enemy see a glimmer of light and bomb the house, there were no reminders of the war inside Mme. Vigny's home, even though she admitted that she had lost both her husband and their only son.

The food, while simple, was delicious. In addition to the soup that had garnered Grant's praises, Mme. Vigny served crusty bread and ended the meal with bowls of stewed apples. The supper was one of the best Emily had eaten since she'd arrived in France, and yet she found her stomach tied in knots. Though the conversation remained casual and Mme. Vigny never again referred to love, the Frenchwoman's gaze continued to move between Emily and Grant, her expression speculative. Clearly, she did not believe Emily's and Grant's protests that they shared nothing more than a desire to reach Maillochauds.

It was with a sense of profound relief that Emily dried the last dish and climbed the stairs to the attic room Mme. Vigny had offered her. Though she had pleaded fatigue from driving on slippery roads, the reason Emily had retired earlier than normal this evening was cowardice. She wanted to escape the Frenchwoman's relentless gaze. While Emily wasn't proud of that, she could not ignore the need to be alone.

And so she stood at the small window, staring at the evening sky. Since she had extinguished all lights, Emily felt safe opening the shutters. The rain had stopped, chased by a strong wind, the same wind that was sending clouds scudding across the moon. Only a few stars were visible through the cloud cover, and the moon itself was obscured most of the time. How fitting, Emily thought. The sky was as clouded as her own thoughts. Though she sought clarity, what she found was confusion.

Mme. Vigny was wrong! Oh, she had been charming as only a Frenchwoman could be, but she was wrong. Emily gripped the windowsill. She wasn't in love with Grant. Of course, she wasn't. She liked him. Even more than that, she cared about him. That was only natural. Grant was a man who'd had a difficult life, yet he'd triumphed over it. Emily admired both his courage and the successes he'd achieved. She worried about him and what the future might hold for him. That was all. Admiration and concern. That was what she felt for Grant.

The moon peeked through its cloud cover, then disappeared again. Emily frowned and tightened her grip on the windowsill. It was true that she admired Grant and worried about him. But if she were being honest with herself, she had to admit that neither admiration nor concern explained the way she reacted every time he touched her. Those undeniable sparks, the warmth that raced up her arm when his fingers brushed against her, were the result of neither admiration nor concern.

There had to be a logical explanation. Emily closed her eyes, trying desperately to find a cause other than the one Mme. Vigny had proposed. It wasn't love. Emily knew that. Love didn't make a person feel as if she'd been punched in the solar plexus when a man smiled at her. Of course it didn't. But then, what was the reason? There had to be one.

Emily's eyes flew open when she heard Beau bark. She looked down and saw that Grant had taken the dog into the yard. Though Beau's dark fur blended into the night, the cast was clearly visible.

Bandages. Wounds. That was it. Emily smiled with relief as she remembered what her sister Carolyn had told her. It was not uncommon, Carolyn had learned in her nurse's training, for patients to believe themselves in love with the nurses who cared for them. The reason had nothing to do with true love and much to do with proximity. There was an enforced closeness in a hospital, not unlike the closeness Emily and Grant had shared as they'd traveled in Hortense. Proximity. That's all it was.

Emily smiled again. It wasn't as if she imagined herself in love with Grant. She did not. She most definitely did not. They were friends and traveling companions, caught up in the most extraordinary adventure of her life. It was normal that she would have strong feelings for him under those circumstances. It would, in fact, be odd if she did not. But love? No. What Emily felt was not love.

Still, she couldn't help wishing that Carolyn were here so that she could talk to her. There were some things even a sister didn't want to put in writing. If she could see Carolyn and talk to her, Emily knew everything would be clear. After all, Carolyn was cap over boots in love with her husband. She would be able to describe love to Emily, and when she did, that would prove once and for all that what Emily felt for Grant was not love.

It couldn't possibly be love.

"It's absurd, Beau." Grant stopped his pacing long enough to stare down at the dog. The animal lay on a pile of rags, and although by all rights he ought to be asleep—as

Grant himself should have been—he kept his eyes fixed on Grant, almost as if he understood his words. "Mme. Vigny might think she's wise," and Grant wouldn't deny the fact that the woman appeared to have an inborn wisdom that exceeded that of many of the best educated men he had met, "but she's wrong about this. Dead wrong."

Grant pivoted on his heel and strode across the floor. When he reached the window, he pivoted again and headed back to the door. He'd paced the floor so many times that he wondered whether the pine planks would soon have ruts worn in them. The repetitive motion was supposed to be soothing. It was supposed to help a man put his thoughts in order. Tonight it was failing, utterly and completely. The more Grant paced, the more agitated he became.

He was not in love with Emily. Heavens, no! Long ago he'd sworn he would never again let himself get attached to another person, much less let himself love someone else. Loving someone was dangerous enough. Being in love was far more serious. Being in love led to promises, to vows that included words like "for richer and poorer, in sickness and in health."

"Those aren't the problem, Beau." The dog laid his muzzle on his paws but kept his eyes focused on Grant. Did the poor creature think Grant and Emily were going to abandon him because of his injury? "I wouldn't do that to you," Grant assured the dog, "any more than I can imagine that my feelings for Emily would change, no matter what kind of malady she contracted." Only a cad would desert a woman under those circumstances, and Grant was not a cad.

"Forsaking all others." That wasn't a problem, either. No woman he'd ever met could compare to Emily, and Grant was certain that even should he live to be as old as Methuselah, he would never find another who did. Not that he would even look. Why would a man do that, when he'd already met the perfect woman? "That would be pretty dumb, wouldn't it, Beau?" The dog blinked.

Grant strode to the window and stared at the closed shutters. He knew what was coming next. The last part of those vows was the one that filled his heart with fear. Though he'd been speaking to Beau, the final words were so awful that he couldn't force them past his lips. "Until death do us part." Oddly, though most of the men he'd met feared death, that wasn't what brought a cold sweat to Grant's forehead. It was the 'parting' part.

Grant had had far too much experience with partings. People left him. Carl and Mickey and the boys he'd known before them. Even animals left. Look at Augustus. He'd stayed with Grant less than a month.

When Beau whimpered, Grant crouched down next to the dog. "Do you think you're different, Beau? You're not." The dog stared at him, and Grant suspected that he understood not a word he'd been saying. Wasn't it true that animals reacted to a person's moods? If so, poor Beau had been the brunt of some pretty vicious moods tonight.

"I know you won't leave until that leg heals," Grant told the dog, "but eventually you'll go. Your place is with Emily." Grant fixed his eyes on the wall, trying not to picture Emily's sweet smile or the joy he'd seen on her face when she'd realized that Beau was still alive.

As the dog's tail thumped on the floor, Grant turned back to him. "I know you accept me because I'm with her, but if you had to choose, you'd be Emily's dog." Beau turned his head in the direction of Emily's room. "See?" Grant's laugh held no mirth. "I can't say that I blame you. I'd make the same choice if I were in your shoes . . . er, paws."

Grant rose and strode to the window. What a ridiculous conversation! The war and Emily's quixotic quest were addling his brains. Look at him, reduced to using a dog as a sounding board. If that wasn't pathetic, Grant wasn't sure what was.

It was all Mme. Vigny's fault. She had raised thoughts that were best left unspoken. Grant didn't love Emily. He couldn't let himself love her, because if he did, he would be utterly destroyed when she left him.

Grant flung himself into the chair and pulled out a sheet of paper. He would write. That was what he always did when his emotions threatened to overwhelm him. Writing was safe. He could pour his emotions onto a piece of paper. Unlike people, words were permanent. Words wouldn't disappear, and no one could take them away. If they weren't warm and soft and if they didn't provide comfort, well . . . a man couldn't have everything. At least words didn't leave gaping holes in his heart.

She called herself the wisest woman in France. Grant started to smile as he remembered Emily's expression when Mme. Vigny had started to expound on Eleanor of Aquitaine and the Courts of Love.

Emily! Drat it all! He wasn't supposed to be thinking about her. He was supposed to be writing a column.

On the surface, she looked like a thousand other French-women. Her gray hair, pulled back into a knot, was as unremarkable as her black clothing. It was only when you saw her eyes that . . .

Grant frowned. The eyes he was picturing were clear blue, the color of an April sky. Mme. Vigny's eyes were brown.

Emily! Why was it that the simplest of references made him conjure her image? Why couldn't he forget her? Grant stared at the paper in front of him, as if it held the answers to his questions. It wasn't because he was in love with Emily. No matter what Mme. Vigny claimed, that wasn't the case.

Grant liked Emily. Of course he did. She was one of the

most likeable people he'd ever met. He even cared about her. He couldn't deny that. He cared about what she would find in Maillochauds. He cared about how she would react if she found her brother changed or, worse, if she found that her brother was no longer alive. It was natural that Grant would care.

But love? That was impossible. And being in love? Preposterous! Simply preposterous.

They were less than a day's drive from Maillochauds now. Emily gripped the steering wheel, uncertain which was stronger, her anticipation or her fear. She wanted to reach Maillochauds. More than anything, she wanted to be reunited with her brother, and yet she could not dismiss her worries. If Theo was alive—and she believed he was—why didn't anyone know? There had to be a reason, but Emily could find no reason that didn't involve serious injury. How she hated the thought of her brother in pain!

"Look for the silver lining, Pollyanna."

Emily turned to stare at Grant. "Was I that obvious?"

He nodded. "White knuckles are a giveaway every time."

"They're not . . ." Emily stopped when she saw that her hands were undeniably pale, the knuckles as light as milk.

"Oh, Grant, I'm such a coward." She pulled the car onto the side of the road and stopped.

"That's one of the most ridiculous things I've ever heard." Grant reached over, tugging her hands until he had clasped them between his. "You don't have a cowardly bone in your body."

His hands were warm, the skin rougher than hers, with a callus on his middle finger from the hours he spent writing. "I've tried everything, but even whistling doesn't help." A gentle breeze wafted the sweet scents of spring through the car. Ordinarily, Emily would have taken comfort from the reminder that this was a season of rebirth.

But this was not an ordinary day. "Even though I'm excited that we're so close, every mile makes me even more anxious."

Grant released her hands, and for a moment Emily felt bereft. Then he reached out and encircled her shoulders with his arm, drawing her closer to him. Only when her head was resting on his shoulder did he speak. "I wish I could help you, Emily, but the truth is, I haven't been able to banish my own fears, even when I whistle in the dark."

Though Emily had sensed that, never before had Grant admitted that he was still plagued with fear. "What are you afraid of?" She couldn't see his face, but she could feel his shoulder stiffening. What had she expected? He wouldn't answer this question, any more than he'd answered the questions about his past.

There was a long silence. Birds sang outside; in the backseat, Beau snored. At last, Grant said simply, "Myself."

"I don't understand. How can you be afraid of yourself?" If Emily had been asked what she thought it was Grant feared, she would not have been able to say. All she knew was, this wasn't what she had expected.

"I'm serious, Emily."

"I know you are." Not even for an instant had she thought otherwise. "I simply don't understand. Help me, please." Suddenly there was nothing more important in the world than learning what it was that Grant feared.

He tightened his grip on her shoulders, and she could feel the strength in his fingers. But physical strength was not the only kind, and Emily knew that Grant was mustering inner resources to voice his fears.

"I have this unfortunate habit of getting attached to people."

"Everyone does that." Emily did not say that most people did not consider it an 'unfortunate habit.'

"But not everyone loses those people. Every . . . single . . . time."

There was such anguish in his voice that she could hardly bear it. Emily twisted so that she could see Grant's face. Though light reflected off his spectacles, it did not obscure the emotion that darkened his eyes.

"Other boys were taken away from the orphanage. They were adopted when you were not." She phrased it as a statement, not a question.

He nodded, and the furrows between his eyes deepened. Suddenly, the pieces to the puzzle that was Grant Randall began to fit together. "Oh, Grant!" Emily laid a hand on his cheek, trying to comfort him.

Grant had said that his childhood in the orphanage had not been horrible. Emily doubted that. For a sensitive boy— and she knew that a man as sensitive as Grant must have been terribly vulnerable as a child—it would have been pure torture. Emily could not imagine what it must have been like, not having a family, not belonging to anyone, then having his only friends wrenched from him. No wonder the man had built a shell around himself.

"I wish I could help you."

Grant shook his head slightly, and she felt the smoothness of his cheek against her palm. "I didn't expect that. Don't worry, Emily. I've long since become reconciled to what I am."

But he hadn't. Grant needed help as much as she did. He might believe he had put his past behind him, but he hadn't. Not at all. The losses Grant had sustained as a child had made him the man he was today, a man who understood the darkness in others' souls, but whose own wounds were still so raw that he wouldn't let anyone close, lest they reopen fully. Grant needed to accept his losses if he was ever going to heal. Emily knew that. A day ago she wouldn't have known what to say, but perhaps she did now.

"While you were outside this morning, I asked Mme. Vigny how she could bear losing her husband and son so close to each other. She gave me some advice."

"From her fount of infinite wisdom?" Though Grant's words were light, the pain Emily had seen in his eyes had not receded.

"Yes." It might not work, but she had to try. Emily spoke slowly, hoping that Grant would listen and that what he heard might help him. At first he stared into the distance, but as she recounted how the Frenchwoman said she kept her loved ones alive in her memory, Emily watched the lines between Grant's eyes fade. When his gaze met hers, the pain was gone, replaced by what appeared to be hope.

"Interesting." Grant's voice was as noncommittal as if he were discussing the weather, not a way of dealing with the losses that had shaped his life. "I might write a column about that." He glanced into the back seat. "As long as we're stopped, I'll take Beau out."

It was vintage Grant. Change the subject. Erect the shield. Keep people from thinking about the man behind the words. Emily sighed as she watched him carry Beau into the grass. The shield was so high and so strong that she wondered if he would ever let anyone behind it for more than a second. And yet, Emily realized, this was twice that Grant had peeled away layers and revealed the depths of his pain. Was it, she wondered, that he was beginning to trust her, or was it simply his way of helping her put her own fears aside for a few minutes?

Grant settled back in the seat and stared out the side window. What a fool he was! Only a fool would have told Emily about Carl and Mickey and Augustus and the way their leaving had hurt him. Only a fool would have admitted that there were some losses that a man never forgot, and some memories that never faded. A wise man would have said nothing, simply let her talk about her fears. But Grant hadn't been wise. He'd spoken without considering the consequences. He could blame it on too little sleep, combined with the desire to help Emily deal with her fears. The truth was, it didn't matter what the reason was. He'd told Emily things that no one else on earth knew. Like Caesar crossing the Rubicon, there was no turning back now. All he could hope was that he wouldn't regret the consequences.

Grant looked at the fields. These were cow pastures, he knew, but since the last offensive, they had been devoid of animals. He had never learned whether the farmers had slaughtered the cattle rather than risk the enemy taking them or whether they were being kept inside a barn. It didn't matter. What mattered was what Grant had revealed to Emily.

Perhaps the consequences wouldn't be too bad. For one thing, Emily had seemed to relax a bit, once he'd gotten her thinking of something other than Theo. She'd been wound up tighter than Grant's watch, and he'd been worried about her. Helping her to relax, if only for a few minutes, could only be good.

Emily deserved a happy ending, like the ones in the fairy tales that she had read as a child. If he could manufacture one, Grant would give it to her. But that was impossible. The truth was, Grant didn't even believe in happy endings. He'd never seen one. Oh, he'd seen endings—plenty of them—but not one had been happy. So how was he to create something that he'd never seen or experienced?

Emily pointed toward the milepost that indicted it was five kilometers to Maillochauds. "Less than an hour now." Her voice was trembling, but somehow her hands were steady on the steering wheel.

"Maybe." Grant tried to inject some humor. "Hortense may have other ideas."

"She wouldn't." Emily's face paled, and Grant regretted his attempt at a joke. He'd hoped to lighten Emily's mood, but instead he'd only added to her worries.

Beau whined, then lurched forward and tried to lick Emily's face.

"Down, boy." Though the dog was trying to comfort Emily, she did not need any further distractions.

When they passed the three kilometer mark, Emily's hands began to tremble. Grant could bear it no longer.

"Stop the car, Emily."

She turned to look at him, her eyes wide with surprise. "Why?"

"I'll show you when we stop." As soon as Hortense was parked, Grant hurried to Emily's side of the car and helped her out. Though she had climbed out of the car unassisted hundreds of times before, Emily was shaking so much that Grant feared she might fall. Perhaps he should have released her hand when she was standing, but Grant had no intention of letting go of Emily. He led her to a smooth stretch of the road, then turned her so she was facing him. Worry etched that beautiful face, and dark circles ringed her eyes.

"You're brave, Emily." Perhaps if he repeated it enough times, she would believe it. "You're the bravest person I know." She stared at him, those lovely blue eyes beginning to well with tears. She didn't believe him, though she needed to. Somehow Grant had to find a way to convince her. "You're strong too. Whatever we find in Maillochauds, I know you'll be able to deal with it." She would. Though she doubted herself, Grant had never met a woman as capable as Emily.

"I wish I were that certain."

Grant reached for her other hand, entwining his fingers with hers. Her fingers were long and slender and surprisingly soft. Though she worked with tools every day, her hands remained almost as smooth as a debutante's.

"I have enough certainty for both of us," Grant told her. The hint of a smile crossed her lips as she absorbed his boast. The smile was a positive step, but Grant needed more. He needed to make her forget what lay ahead. He needed to give her a memory to hold close, no matter what she found in Maillochauds.

"I want to give you one more thing," he said.

She raised a brow. "What is that?"

"A kiss for good luck." And before she could react, he drew her into his arms and lowered his lips to hers. It was supposed to be a casual gesture, the lightest of kisses, nothing more than a brief touching of lips. That was what he had intended. But that was before he had tasted Emily's lips. That was before he had realized that they were soft and sweet and that he never, ever wanted to let them go.

"Oh, Emily!" Grant murmured, and he drew her closer.

Chapter Eleven

There was nothing special about Maillochauds. Emily tried to fight back her disappointment as she steered Hortense into the center of the small town. Perhaps it was foolish, but she had clung to the hope that when she reached the place that sheltered Theo, she would feel a special pull, something to confirm her belief that her brother was here. Instead she felt nothing other than a sense of disbelief that she had traveled so far and that her destination was so ordinary.

Emily had believed that Maillochauds would look different from the other villages she and Grant had seen. It did not. Like many towns in this part of France, the main road led to a central square. There the road diverged, forcing a visitor to choose either the right or the left side of the grassy plot that marked the middle of the town.

Emily depressed the clutch and brake pedals to stop the car. No matter how unimpressive the town was, they had arrived. The next exploration would be done on foot. She closed the coil switch, then looked around. The central square of many towns boasted a statue. Maillochauds was no exception. Not only did it have a statue, but that statue

145

was perched on top of a fountain. Though it should have been a pretty sight, it was not. Emily suspected that in happier times, water would cascade into the base, the soothing sounds of splashing masking the noises of ordinary life. But these were not happier times, and the fountain remained silent, the water coated with green algae. Even sadder, the statue was missing its head. ANGEL OF HOPE, the placard at the foot of the statue declared. *Please*, Emily prayed silently, *don't let this be an omen*. Surely hope could not be destroyed as easily as a stone statue. She would not give up hope. Theo was here; he had to be.

"Where do you want to start?" Grant stood next to her. Though he did not touch her, he was close enough that Emily could feel the warmth of his body, and that reminded her of how good it had felt to be held in his arms. Grant believed that she was brave; he believed that she was strong. She couldn't disappoint him.

Emily looked at the gray stone buildings that flanked the square. While several had boarded up windows, undoubtedly the result of the same shelling that had destroyed the angel's head, a few shopkeepers had unfurled their brightly colored awnings, bravely announcing to the world that they were still in business.

She pointed toward the greengrocer. Not only was his green and white striped awning the newest, but his door was open. It was, she told herself, a good omen. She wouldn't think about the statue. Instead she would believe that the kiss Grant had given her had brought luck, just as he'd promised. Hortense had suffered no breakdowns; they had reached Maillochauds before nightfall; at least one shop was open. All of those were proof of good luck, and she had Grant to thank for them.

Emily touched her fingers to her lips, remembering how sweet the kiss had been. Never, not even in her dreams, had she realized that anything could be so wonderful. When he'd touched his lips to hers, Emily had felt sparks, and then the warmth had started. It had begun in her fingertips, quickly moving up her arms, then traveling down her body, setting each of her nerve endings on fire. Nothing had ever felt so good. For a few moments, Emily had felt safe and, even more, she had felt cherished. It was all an illusion, of course. Grant had intended nothing other than a kiss for luck. But for Emily, it had been much more. It had been the sweetest thing that had ever happened to her, a moment that she would remember for the rest of her life. No matter what she found here in Maillochauds, she would have the memory of Grant's kiss.

Emily looked up at him. Those brown eyes that had smiled at her so warmly less than an hour earlier were now solemn. "It'll be all right," Grant said.

Emily wished she were so confident. "Let's get started." They left Beau in Hortense's back seat, admonishing him to remain there until they returned. Though the dog whined and put his muzzle on the windowsill, he made no effort to climb out of the car.

The afternoon was still warm, and the fresh scents of spring perfumed the air. Though the battle had once raged only kilometers away, the sounds of war were no longer audible. Maillochauds was as peaceful a town as Emily had seen anywhere in France. If Theo was here, he was safe. Unfortunately, that did nothing to quell the trembling in her legs. She took a deep breath, then entered the shop.

"I'm sorry, mademoiselle," the gray-haired proprietor said when Emily had asked him about Theo. "We have no strangers here."

Emily stared at the man, not wanting to believe him, but even when Grant repeated the question, the answer was the same.

"He's lying," Emily said when she and Grant had left the shop and were out of earshot. "He knows something."

Her trembling had increased, fueled by anger as well as fear.

Grant tucked her hand into his arm as they walked along the narrow sidewalk. Though they had agreed that they would stop in every store, then continue their inquiries at private residences if needed, Grant seemed to sense that Emily was not yet ready to face another shopkeeper. "What makes you think that?" he asked. "I thought the man was telling the truth."

He wasn't. Emily was sure of that. "He wouldn't meet my gaze," she told Grant. The shopkeeper had stared past her, apparently looking at the display in his plate glass window. In Emily's experience, a person did that when he didn't want to reveal his thoughts.

"I noticed that," Grant admitted, "but there could be another reason. Perhaps the man was uncomfortable with you."

As they crossed the street, Emily looked both ways. There were no other pedestrians. Although several shop doors were open, no one strolled the sidewalk.

"Why would he not be comfortable with me?" Emily didn't consider herself a threatening person, even though she stood two inches taller than the shopkeeper.

"It could be that he was shy." When Emily raised one eyebrow, encouraging Grant to continue, he said, "Beautiful young women aren't very common here, and beautiful young American women are even less common."

He thought she was beautiful! She wasn't, of course, but despite that, Grant's words sent a flush of color to her cheeks. Emily closed her eyes for a second, willing herself to stop blushing. This was just another example of Grant's kindness. First the kiss for good luck, then the arm that supported her and helped ease the trembling, now this. Grant's goal was to lessen Emily's fears by making her think of something other than Theo for a moment or two.

It was, she had to admit, an effective strategy. Now that her legs were no longer threatening to collapse, it was time to continue on their quest.

"Let's ask someone else. The greengrocer is not the only man in town."

Half an hour later, when they'd spoken to each of the shopkeepers on the central square and had received the same negative response, Grant nodded slowly. "I think you're right," he admitted as they headed back to the car. "Theo's here, and everyone is protecting him."

"From his sister?"

Grant shrugged. "It's wartime, Emily. They may fear that we're spies for the enemy. If they admitted to harboring an American, there could be reprisals against the whole town."

Though Emily hated the thought, she knew there was truth to Grant's words. The villagers could be protecting themselves as well as Theo. "I'm not going to give up. I haven't come this far to admit defeat so easily." If she had to, Emily would go to every house in the town, looking for her brother. If everyone denied that he was there, she would repeat the process tomorrow and each day after that until someone admitted he had seen Theo. Her brother was in Maillochauds; Emily was confident of that. All she needed to do was find him.

As they approached the car, Beau woofed.

"All right, boy. We can let you play for a minute or two." Grant opened the door and helped the dog out of the car. For the past few days, Grant had allowed Beau to try to walk. Though the dog's awkwardness and the inevitable falls wrenched Emily's heart, Grant had assured her that it would keep Beau's muscles from weakening.

Grant settled the dog on the ground, then moved a few feet away, encouraging him to come to him. At the same time, a small child and his mother emerged from the greengrocer's. Emily stared at them in surprise. They must have entered the store while she and Grant were in one of the shops on the other side of the square.

The little boy's eyes widened when he saw the dog. "*Maman*, look!" he cried as Beau hobbled. "Do you think the enemy hurt him?"

As tears welled in the child's eyes, Emily realized how deeply the war had affected everyone in Maillochauds. If a boy as young as this lived with fear, it was no wonder no one wanted to risk their lives by admitting that someone in the village harbored Theo.

Before the Frenchwoman could reply, Emily spoke. "Beau is a very brave dog," she told the child. "The gentleman and I were hungry," she said with a brief nod at Grant. "Beau was chasing a rabbit so we could have dinner. Unfortunately, he got his leg caught in a snare."

The boy nodded, his relief that the dog was not a war casualty evident. For a moment, he watched Beau's efforts, then he turned his eyes toward Emily. He squinted at her and tipped his head to one side, the picture of concentration. At first, lines formed between his eyes. "You look like someone," he said, and the lines deepened. Then he grinned. "The poor man. That's it. You look like the poor man," he announced, his voice triumphant.

Emily caught her breath. "What man?" There was only one man she resembled.

As Beau hobbled toward her, Grant closed the distance and stood at her side. Though he no longer touched her, Emily knew he was ready to provide whatever support she needed. It was clear from Grant's expression that he knew, as she did, that what the little boy was about to tell them was important. It was equally clear that Grant wanted to share the moment with her. Emily nodded. They had traveled so far together. It was right that Grant was with her now.

The boy kept his eyes fixed on Emily. "You look like

the man who's staying with Jeanne-Claude and her *maman*." His voice was clear, his earlier confusion gone.

"*Tais toi*, Philippe." The Frenchwoman put her hand on her son's shoulder, but it was too late to urge him to be quiet. He had already told Emily what she needed to know. Theo was here! Somewhere in this small town was a woman named Jeanne-Claude, and wherever she was, Emily would find her brother. No matter what the Army believed, Theo was still alive.

"Please, madame," Emily pleaded. "You must be able to see that the man is my brother. We're twins." Emily turned to Grant, confirming that she had used the correct word. "*Jumeaux*," she repeated. When the woman nodded, Emily continued, "I need to find him." The fact that Philippe had referred to Theo as 'the poor man' confirmed what Emily had feared, that Theo had been wounded. Though her heart ached at the thought that her brother was in pain, at the same time she rejoiced in the knowledge that he was alive.

The woman was silent for a long moment. Then, her reluctance evident, she gave Emily directions to a house on the outskirts of the town. "If the American is your brother," the Frenchwoman said, "that is where he's staying." She took her son's hand and hurried into the next store.

"Oh, Grant!" Emily could not stop smiling. "I knew he was here!" She continued to smile as she drove the short distance to the woman named Jeanne-Claude's house.

"Do you want me to come in with you?" Grant asked.

Emily nodded. Just as it had seemed right that Grant be at her side when little Philippe revealed that Theo was here, it seemed right that Grant accompany her on this the ultimate stage of their journey. "Please," she said simply as she gripped the steering wheel, trying to contain her excitement. In just a few minutes, she would be reunited with Theo. In just a few minutes, she would have proof that the War Office was wrong and that her brother was alive.

Jeanne-Claude's home was as unremarkable as the town itself. Built of gray stone with a slate roof, it resembled dozens of other houses that Emily had seen. Only the brightly colored pansies growing next to the foundation distinguished this house from the others.

Emily stared at the small cottage for a moment, suddenly unable to move. Now that Theo was only yards away, though she was anxious to see him, a fear greater than any she had ever known swept through her. What if Theo wasn't here? What if he was changed beyond recognition?

"Try whistling." Grant reached across the car and laid his hand on top of Emily's. The warmth of his touch broke through her paralysis and she nodded. Grant was right. She needed to confront her fears. She needed to find Theo.

Emily climbed down from the car and started to walk toward the house. Though Grant was at her side, he said nothing, as if he knew that she needed silence. Emily stared at the building where Theo was reported to be. No larger than the Ferrands', she guessed that it contained only two or three rooms. Was there a root cellar? Was that where the woman named Jeanne-Claude kept Theo hidden? Was that why darkness had frightened Emily? Soon she would have her answers.

Emily knocked on the door. There was no answer. Though the plume of smoke revealed that the house was inhabited, it appeared that Jeanne-Claude and her mother were not willing to open the door to strangers. Emily knocked again. This time she heard footsteps. A few seconds later, the door was opened a crack. The woman who stood in the opening was of medium height with the dark brown hair and eyes so common in this part of France.

"Are you Jeanne-Claude?"

The flicker of recognition that had lit the Frenchwoman's eyes when she saw Emily was quickly extinguished. "Yes," she admitted. "I'm Jeanne-Claude Fignon." Jeanne-Claude kept her hand on the edge of the door, as if preparing to close it in Emily's face.

Emily spoke quickly. "I've come to see my brother. Theo Wentworth," she added.

Though Emily would have sworn that the woman recognized the name, she shook her head. "I beg your pardon, mademoiselle. You must be mistaken. There's no one here by that name."

As Emily shook her own head, Grant took her hand in his, silently reminding her that she was not alone. "The villagers tried to protect you," Emily told Jeanne-Claude, "but little Philippe recognized me. He saw what you must— that Theo is my twin."

Jeanne-Claude shook her head again. "I regret . . ."

As she started to close the door, a man called out, "Who's there, Jeanne-Claude?" There was no mistaking Theo's voice. Emily's heart skipped a beat. Theo was alive, he was here, and he sounded perfectly normal. Perhaps her worries had been for naught.

"It's no one important," the Frenchwoman lied. "Just a stranger asking for directions."

Though Jeanne-Claude tried to close the door, Emily lodged her foot in the opening. Theo was here, and she was going to see him. This woman who was blocking the door would not succeed in keeping Emily from her brother.

"I thought I heard Emily."

While Jeanne-Claude was distracted by Theo's words, Emily brushed past her, following the sound of her brother's voice. "Let her go," she heard Grant say to the Frenchwoman.

The cottage was small. A single room served as both dining room and parlor, with a tiny kitchen alcove on one side. On the opposite wall, two doors led to what Emily assumed were bedrooms. Theo was in the one on the right.

"You did hear me, Theo. You did!" She ran into the

room, unable to contain her excitement. The journey was
over. She had found her brother. But as she entered the
room, Emily stopped abruptly, her excitement tempered
with shock. Theo was here. That was true. The journey was
over. That was also true. But the ending was not the one
she had envisioned.

Her brother sat in a chair next to the room's sole window, dressed in garments Emily had never seen. The dark
trousers and blue shirt were not part of his uniform, nor
were they clothes he had worn at home as a civilian. Instead, they appeared to be the clothing of a French farmer.
Perhaps Jeanne-Claude thought he would be less conspicuous if he wore French clothing, not realizing that Theo's
height and blond hair would mark him as a foreigner.

Still, it was not the clothing that shocked Emily and
made her heart pound with fear. Her brother's right hand
was encased in a cast, and an angry red scar marred his
once perfect face. It was obvious that Theo was still re-
covering from some of his wounds. As for the others . . .
Emily closed her eyes for a second as she realized why she
had dreamed of darkness. Though sun streamed through the
window, spilling onto the bed and the small expanse of
floor, Theo could not see it, for a wide white bandage cir-
cled his head, covering his eyes.

Emily took a deep breath. There could be many reasons
why Theo's eyes were bandaged. It didn't have to be what
she feared. Emily crossed the room in three quick strides,
then knelt next to Theo's chair and took his uninjured hand
in hers. "Oh, Theo, it's so good to see you!" The instant
the words were out of Emily's mouth, she regretted them.
How insensitive could she be?

"*Mon cher*, are you all right?" Jeanne-Claude appeared
in the doorway, concern etching her face. "Do you want
her to leave?"

Grant stood next to Jeanne-Claude, his expression clearly

asking Emily if she wanted him to join her. She shook her head slowly. This was something she had to do alone.

Theo shook his head. "Please give us a few minutes together." When Jeanne-Claude had left, closing the door behind her and Grant, Theo stared in Emily's direction. "Is it really you, Emily? What are you doing in France?"

Emily realized that, just as the family had had no word from Theo, he had no way of knowing what had happened to them since he'd been reported killed. "We heard that your entire battalion was lost in the battle. The War Office was convinced that you were with them, but I wouldn't believe them. That's why I convinced the Army they should let me drive an ambulance."

A hint of a smile crossed Theo's face. "That sounds like you." He tightened his grip on her hand. "I figured the Army would come. I never thought they'd send you."

It didn't make sense. "They didn't send me, Theo. No one knows you're here."

A puzzled expression crossed the face she knew almost as well as her own. "I don't understand." Theo shrugged. "I was in pretty bad shape at first. The grenade broke my jaw and right hand." Emily noted that Theo did not mention the damage to his eyes. "For weeks I couldn't speak or write or . . ." Again he did not complete the sentence. "But the wires came out of my jaw two weeks ago. Jeanne-Claude sent a telegram to the Army the first day I could speak. I know she did."

"Then they'll be here soon. I'll see if they'll let me go home with you."

Theo shook his head. "I don't want to go home."

Emily stared. "I don't understand. Why don't you want to go home?"

"Surely that should be obvious."

"Your eyes." That was the only reason Emily could imagine. But even then she didn't understand it. At home

Theo would be with people who loved him. At home there were excellent doctors. "It's only temporary," she said, as much to convince herself as to reassure her brother.

"The doctor wasn't sure," Theo admitted, "but he thinks there's little chance I'll regain my sight. I can't go home like this."

This was her brother, her twin, her lifelong friend. Emily knew him almost as well as she did herself. Until a few minutes ago, she had thought she knew how he would react to every situation. But this Theo was a man she had never before met. Was this what Grant had tried to tell her, that war scarred men emotionally as well as physically? Surely Theo could see that there was a silver lining, no matter how dark the clouds appeared to be.

"You're alive, Theo. That's all that matters." Emily thought of the joy that Carolyn and Martha would share when they learned that their brother had not been killed. In this terrible war, where far too many men had died, their brother was still alive. That was little short of a miracle.

Theo tried to pull his hand from Emily's, but she tightened her grip. "You wouldn't think it was all that mattered," he said, "if you were sitting here." Theo dropped his chin to his chest, then raised it again, almost defiantly. "There are days when I think I would have been better off if I had died with the rest of my battalion."

"Don't say that!" Tears sprang to Emily's eyes. "It's a miracle that you're alive."

Theo shook his head. "Half alive. That's all I am." He tugged his hand free and grabbed the arm of the chair. "What good is a blind man?" Before Emily could speak, Theo continued, "I'll tell you, Emily. He's no good at all."

"You're wrong."

"And you're a Pollyanna. Can't you understand? I don't want anyone to see me like this. It's bad enough that Jeanne-Claude is saddled with me."

There was a note in Theo's voice that Emily had never before heard, and she wondered what had caused it.

"Jeanne-Claude seems very protective of you," Emily told her brother.

He frowned again. "It's pity, nothing more." Theo turned to face the window, leaving Emily with a view of his back. "I think you'd better leave now."

Emily's protests met only silence. Finally, tears streaming down her face, she rushed out of the room.

"I'm so worried," she told Grant when they were back in the car. Beau whined and tried to lick her face. Though Theo had told her to leave, Emily had no intention of doing so. She was not leaving Maillochauds without her brother. Somehow she would convince the Army to let her take him home. And once home, she would find the best doctors in the land.

"First we need to tell the Army where Theo is," Grant said when she explained her plan.

Emily blinked back her tears. "Jeanne-Claude notified them."

Grant shook his head. "No, she didn't. She told Theo she had sent the telegram, but she never did."

"Why not? Didn't she realize we thought he was dead?"

Grant's eyes were somber. "I don't think she thought that far. I suspect she wanted to keep Theo safe, and that was her way."

"Her way was wrong." Emily thought of the pain her sisters had endured. How could Jeanne-Claude deprive them of the joy of knowing Theo was alive? "Doesn't she know that we love him?"

When Grant spoke, his words were soft. "Perhaps she loves him too."

Emily stared at Grant. "Did she say that?" Emily shouldn't have been surprised that while the Frenchwoman would barely speak to her, she had shared personal confidences with Grant. The man was a master at drawing information from people.

"She didn't have to. It was obvious from the way she spoke." Grant gestured to one of the buildings on the center square. "Let me send the telegram. By tonight, your sisters should know that Theo's here."

While they were eating supper in the town's one hotel, Emily laid down her fork. "I don't understand. Theo was always the happiest of us children. It didn't take much to make him laugh, and when he wasn't laughing at something else, he was trying to make us laugh. And now . . ." Her brother's despair worried her more than the fact that he was blind.

Behind his spectacles, Grant's eyes were solemn. "Your brother's been dealt an enormous blow."

Didn't he think she knew that? "Blind people can lead good lives," Emily said. There had been a blind woman in Canela who had amazed her neighbors by continuing to crochet intricate doilies, even after she lost her sight.

"That's true," Grant agreed, "but it's a life with many limitations. That's what Theo's fighting now." Emily looked at Grant as she reached for a piece of bread. His expression was almost as bleak as Theo's had been. "Your brother lost more than his eyesight. He lost his dream of having a normal life."

Grant spoke with such assurance that Emily wondered where he'd gained his insights. "Is that what you've learned from interviewing other wounded men?" she asked.

Grant shook his head. "I could claim that was the case, but the truth is, I learned it firsthand." He stared out the window for a moment, then turned to face Emily again. "When I was young, I used to dream of being like other boys. Every night, I prayed that someone would adopt me." Though his voice was even, Grant was unable to disguise the pain, and it wrenched Emily's heart as deeply as Theo's unhappiness had. "It never happened. At first when the prospective parents came, no one wanted a child with poor eyesight. Then they wanted younger boys." The way Grant clenched his fists told Emily that the hurt he'd endured was still an open wound. "Eventually I learned not to dream."

Emily's heart ached for the boy who'd been rejected, the boy who'd turned into a man without dreams. Grant deserved so much more. Though she had been unable to help her brother today, perhaps she could say something that would begin to heal Grant's wounds. Perhaps she could help him, as he had helped her so many times.

"You've accomplished so much," Emily told Grant. Suddenly it became vital that he believe her. "You've touched so many people's lives with your writing." His words had given readers the hope he claimed he didn't believe in. "You've made people smile on the darkest days. Oh, Grant, can't you see how much you've done?"

Grant's lips tightened with what appeared to be anger. "Don't pity me, Emily." His voice was harsh. "I don't want your pity."

Something inside Emily snapped. Perhaps it was the result of all the strain. Perhaps it was simply the culmination of weeks of worry. Emily didn't know. All she knew was that Grant's rejection unleashed her own anger. It was too much. The two men she cared most about were both blind, one in reality, the other figuratively. Neither one of them could see the truth. They didn't understand that a woman was capable of feeling more than pity. They were so blind that they rejected the most precious gift anyone could offer.

Emily reached across the table and grabbed Grant's arm. "Pity. Is that what you think I feel for you?" she demanded. When he did not answer, she continued, her voice low and angry. "You're wrong, Grant. I don't pity you. I love you."

Chapter Twelve

He was sitting in the same chair, wearing the same clothes, his face bearing the same desolate expression she had seen the day before. If it weren't for the fact that some-one—probably Jeanne-Claude—had trimmed his hair, Emily could have believed that her brother had not moved an inch since yesterday, whereas Grant . . . Emily forced that thought away. She would think about Theo's stubbornness, his haircut, anything other than the way Grant had reacted to her declaration of love. The man had stared at her as if she'd suddenly sprouted a second nose. Then he had turned away, and though he had spoken of other things, not once had he referred to the words that had been wrenched from Emily's heart.

"I thought you were leaving." Though Theo did not smile, his voice sounded happier than yesterday. Emily took that as a good omen. Perhaps Theo would be more reasonable than the man she loved. Perhaps his fears would be easier to overcome than Grant's.

"Didn't you learn anything when we were growing up?" Emily demanded. Theo couldn't see it, but she put her hands on her hips and frowned at him in imitation of their mother when they'd annoyed her. "It's not that easy to get rid of me."

Perhaps he sensed what she was doing. Perhaps it was simply her light tone. Emily didn't know what caused it, but she wasn't arguing with the results. Theo laughed. It wasn't a full-fledged laugh. Instead, it sounded as if laughter were a skill he had to relearn. Emily didn't care. This was progress.

"You mean like the day you hid in the hedge, because you wanted to see what Ed Bleeker and I were doing?" Theo asked. His lips curved into a smile, and the deep lines that bracketed his mouth disappeared as he remembered one of the more ignominious episodes of Emily's childhood.

Through the open door Emily heard the clink of china on wood and the sound of soft voices. Jeanne-Claude's mother had greeted Emily and Grant, then returned to her garden. Though Jeanne-Claude's reluctance to leave Theo had been obvious, she had allowed Emily to enter her brother's room alone. Judging from the sounds, Jeanne-Claude and Grant were sharing coffee and conversation. That was nice, but what truly mattered was Theo and the smile that lit his face.

Seeing that smile, Emily felt as if she'd been battling against an invincible foe and suddenly, without warning, she had vanquished the enemy. The war might not be over, but surely it had reached a turning point. She wouldn't say anything. She wouldn't let Theo know what his smile meant to her. Not now, when his mood seemed precariously balanced between despair and hope. She would simply try to sustain his smile. Emily kept her own tone light.

"You would remind me of that, wouldn't you? I was so sure I was going to learn some deep, dark secrets of boyhood that day, but all I discovered was that the hedge had thorns." Emily chuckled, remembering their mother's reaction when she saw the scratches on Emily's arms and legs. Mother had spread salve on the scratches while she pointed out that eavesdropping was often a painful experience.

"Did you really think I'd leave you out if it was something important?" Theo was leaning forward now, his arms resting on his knees. If it weren't for the bandage covering his eyes, Emily could have believed they were back in Canela, reminiscing about their childhood.

She nodded, then realized that Theo couldn't see her gesture. "I thought you and Ed had some kind of fraternity that I couldn't join because I was a girl."

Theo laughed, and this time there was nothing tentative about it. "Never that. Emily," he said as he tried to control his mirth, "you're the most resourceful girl I've ever met."

"Thanks for the compliment . . . if it was one."

"Oh, it was." Theo's face sobered, and he was silent for a moment. When he spoke, his words surprised Emily. "Remember how we always said we'd help each other?" Emily nodded again. That was the reason she had come to Maillochauds, to help her brother. He clenched his jaw in a gesture Emily knew meant he was weighing his words carefully. Theo swallowed, then said, "There's something you can do for me."

"Anything." Emily answered without hesitation. Theo was her brother, her twin, her best friend. There was nothing on earth she would not do for him.

He leaned forward again, stretching his uninjured hand toward her. When she placed her right hand in his, Theo gripped it. "Promise me you'll tell the truth."

"I will." A tremor of fear swept through Emily. What could be so important to Theo? His demeanor made her fear that it was a matter of life and death.

He relaxed his grip on her hand slightly, but his expression remained intent. "Describe Jeanne-Claude to me."

For a second Emily was tempted to laugh. This was what Theo considered vital? But as she looked at her brother's face, she knew that he awaited her answer as eagerly as he must have awaited the doctor's prognosis of his sight.

"She's about four inches shorter than me," Emily said, "but you probably know that." If, as she suspected, Jeanne-Claude had helped Theo to walk, he would be aware of her height and the fact that she was slim. "Her hair is brown, but not as dark as some Frenchwomen's. I'd say it's almost the same shade as a pecan."

Emily continued her description, watching her brother's face intently as she spoke. It was frustrating, not being able to see his eyes, but even without that, she watched his lips curve into a smile unlike any she had ever seen. This was the man she'd known her whole life. Until he'd left for war, they'd never been parted, and they'd accepted the fact that they knew each other better than anyone else could. They'd shared hopes and dreams, hurts and disappointments. Emily had seen her brother shout in triumph, groan with pain, smile with happiness. But she had never before seen him look like this.

"You love her, don't you?" The words slipped out seemingly of their own volition. Emily heard laughter in the kitchen. She wasn't laughing. She was waiting for Theo's reply, knowing that his answer could change not just his life but also hers.

Theo's lips tightened. "No. Yes." He frowned, and for a second Emily thought he would refuse to say anything more. Then he spoke. "It's more than love, Emily. I've fallen *in love* with Jeanne-Claude."

"Wonderful!" To Emily's relief, her voice sounded normal, and Theo could not see that the smile she gave him was bittersweet. Though Emily rejoiced that her brother had found love in the midst of this horrible war, her joy was tempered by the knowledge that their lives would never again be the same.

Theo had changed. While nothing would destroy the special tie that they shared as twins, that connection had already begun to diminish in importance as he entered the next phase of his life. As children, they had been inseparable. And now? In the space of a few months, Theo had found someone who was more important to him than Emily. He had found the woman with whom he wanted to spend the rest of his life, a woman who would fill a spot in his heart that no sister ever could. Theo had changed, while Emily . . .

She paused, trying to find the right word. Perhaps she had changed too. She thought back over the past months and realized that she was no longer the same Emily Wentworth who had come to France. Her journey to find Theo had forced her to rely on herself in ways she had never had before. She was stronger and more independent than she had been in Canela. For the first time in her life she was Emily—just Emily, not Theo's twin. Grant had taught her that.

Grant. Emily took a deep breath. She wouldn't think about him right now. She wouldn't let herself think about the fact that he had dismissed her declaration of love, ignoring it as if it were of no more importance than last night's dinner. Emily leaned forward and wrapped her arms around her brother.

"It's wonderful that you're in love," she repeated, and this time her smile was filled with happiness for Theo and the joy he'd found. A month ago, she might have been hurt by the knowledge that she was no longer the most important person in his life. Now it seemed not just inevitable but right that their lives were diverging. If Jeanne-Claude could bring Theo happiness, if she could turn his despair to hope, Emily would be thrilled.

Theo shook his head as he pushed Emily away. "It's not wonderful. It's horrible."

Emily settled back in her chair, trying not to be hurt by his rejection, trying not to remember how Grant had rejected her. This time it wasn't personal, she told herself. Theo was confused and hurt as he tried to rebuild his life in a world that had changed in ways neither of them could have imagined.

"How can love be horrible?" Emily demanded. Love was what brought beauty and happiness to the world. Love was what would help her brother deal with his possible blindness. It was everything that was good and kind. It was *not* horrible.

The sun broke through the clouds, flooding the room with light. Emily blinked at the sudden brightness, then bit her lips at the realization that Theo might never again see the sun. He could feel its warmth and smell the changes it made in the flowers and grass, but he might not see the golden rays that sparkled with dust motes.

Though her own heart filled with grief, she knew his blindness was not the reason Theo's face contorted with pain. "I love Jeanne-Claude more than I thought it possible to love anyone. She's everything I ever wanted in a woman," he said in a voice so low Emily had to strain to hear it. "That's the problem," Theo continued. "Jeanne-Claude has everything to offer a man, while I have nothing to give her in return."

Emily's heart went out to her brother, for his voice was once more filled with the hopelessness she had heard in it yesterday. Though she had been unable to help him then, she couldn't let that stop her from trying again. Love, she knew, needed to be given, even if the gift was refused. And maybe—just maybe—Theo would be luckier than she.

"You're wrong, Theo. You have something to give to

Jeanne-Claude. You love her. That's more than something. It's everything!"

Theo shook his head, and his lips twisted into a frown. "You don't understand. I won't be a burden to anyone— especially not Jeanne-Claude."

Emily did understand Theo's fears. As the most inde- pendent of the Wentworth siblings, it must be difficult for him to have to rely on someone else for the most basic of needs. Emily did not blame Theo for his fears. Anyone could be afraid. But Theo was wrong to be afraid. This time his fears were groundless. "If Jeanne-Claude loves you, you won't be a burden," Emily told her brother.

"She doesn't love me." Theo's words rang with despair.

"How do you know? Have you asked her?" Grant was sure that Jeanne-Claude loved Theo, and Emily agreed with him. She had seen the way Jeanne-Claude looked at her brother. When she did, the lovely Frenchwoman had worn the same expression that Emily had seen on Theo's face when he'd spoken of the woman who now claimed his heart.

"No."

He hadn't told Jeanne-Claude of his love. How foolish! Surely if the war had taught him anything, it should have been to seize happiness wherever he could find it. "Why not?"

Emily recognized the mulish expression on Theo's face. He had made up his mind, and nothing was going to change it.

"I'm afraid to ask her," Theo admitted. "What would I say?" He paused for a moment, and when he spoke, his voice bore an imitation British accent. "I say, old dear, I love you, and it would be jolly good if you loved me too." Returning to his normal voice, Theo asked, "Do you think she'd like that?"

If the situation hadn't been so serious, Emily would have

smiled. This was the old Theo, trying to make others laugh by making fun of himself. For the first time, Emily realized that when he'd done that, Theo had been trying to defeat his own fears. "You don't need to be ashamed of being afraid," she told him. "We're all afraid of something. The important thing is to conquer those fears." She paused for a second, then said, "When I was afraid that I wouldn't reach you in time, Grant taught me to fight my fears by whistling in the dark."

Theo's lips thinned, and Emily knew that if she could have seen his eyes, she would have seen a glare reflected in them. "Whistling in the dark. That's a great suggestion." Theo's laugh held no mirth. "Isn't it fortunate that I'll have so many opportunities to whistle in the dark? After all, I know how to whistle, and I may have to live in permanent darkness."

She couldn't let him continue to be mired in self-pity. "Stop feeling sorry for yourself." Emily's words were harsh, designed to jolt her brother into reasonableness.

They hit their mark, for a flush stained his cheeks. Theo rose and pointed toward the door. "Give it up, Emily. I'm a hopeless cause."

"Let me get you some more coffee, Monsieur Randall." The Frenchwoman gestured toward the china pot that sat on the table between them. When Grant had escorted Emily back to the cottage, Jeanne-Claude had suggested that he join her for a cup of coffee.

"Thank you, but please call me Grant."

Jeanne-Claude nodded. "Certainly, Grant." She looked down at the floor where Beau slept. Though the dog had wanted to follow Emily into her brother's room, Jeanne-Claude had suggested he remain here, telling Emily that Theo was especially sensitive to odors. "Your dog needs a bath," she had said, causing both Emily and Grant to grin.

"When we're finished with the coffee, I'll show you the wagon." She had told Grant about a wooden wagon that her father had used to transport vegetables into the center of the village. "Your poor dog might like a ride."

Grant nodded. "The day is too beautiful to be spent indoors."

"On that we all agree. All except for Theo." The Frenchwoman's lovely face bore a wry smile as she refilled her coffee cup. "He's the most stubborn man I've ever met—probably the most stubborn man on earth."

Grant couldn't help smiling. "His sister isn't much better. Once Emily gets an idea, nothing can dissuade her."

Jeanne-Claude took a sip of the delicious brew, then nodded sagely. "Ah, but we love them, anyway, don't we?"

Love? Grant blinked in surprise. Love? What on earth did the woman mean? And why was she looking at him as if she expected him to agree? It was preposterous. Grant raised his cup and took another sip of coffee. Surely she wouldn't expect him to speak when his mouth was full.

Jeanne-Claude laughed, and the sound reminded him of a mountain stream. It was soft and musical and made a man want to smile. Or it would, if the subject hadn't been so ridiculous.

"Don't look so shocked," she said. "Did you think it wasn't obvious?"

The woman was speaking perfect French. Grant understood every word. And yet they made no sense.

"I don't know what you mean."

Jeanne-Claude laughed again. "Love," she said, as if that explained everything. "It's obvious that you love Emily the way I love Theo—utterly, completely and forever."

Had the woman taken leave of her senses? Grant didn't doubt that she loved Emily's brother. Even a man with eyesight as poor as Grant's could see that. But Grant and Emily? Nonsense! "I don't love Emily." It was annoying the way his voice cracked, almost as if he were lying. He wasn't. He didn't love Emily, and she didn't love him. Oh, she had said she did, but that had been her temper speaking. People said things in the heat of anger that they didn't mean. Emily had been trying to shock him out of his mood. She'd succeeded, both in shocking him and in changing his mood. But now that her temper had cooled, she would realize that she hadn't meant what she'd said.

She didn't love him. Of course she didn't. And that wonderful feeling of warmth, the sense that he was not alone in the world, had faded along with the realization that Emily hadn't meant anything by those three words. If she loved him—and Grant doubted that she did—it was the kind of love she felt for her brother. It wasn't real love, not the kind Jeanne-Claude meant.

Jeanne-Claude tapped her finger on the table, demanding Grant's attention. "You can't fool me," she said, her brown eyes sparkling with mirth. "I'm a Frenchwoman, and I recognize love." She smiled again. "It's as unmistakable as the measles."

Grant made a show of inspecting his hands. "I don't see any spots," he announced.

"Ah, Grant." Jeanne-Claude shook her head slowly. "You can laugh all you want, but that won't change it. You're in love with Emily."

Why was it that these Frenchwomen thought of nothing but love? "You're the second woman who's told me that," he admitted.

"Aha!" Jeanne-Claude's smile was filled with triumph. "That's because it's true."

Grant rose and walked to the window, trying to marshal his thoughts. It couldn't be true. It couldn't possibly have happened. Years ago he had vowed that he would not let himself love, for to love was to risk his heart, and he would never again let himself be so vulnerable.

A cloud scudded across the sky, momentarily blocking the sun, casting a long shadow on the ground. Grant knew about shadows. He'd lived with them his whole life. Shadows were the fears that threatened you at night, the knowledge that nothing was permanent, that everyone left. Shadows were the pain of waking each morning, knowing you'd never see your friend again. It had happened over and over again. Carl, Mickey, Augustus. At the time, the loss had been so intense that Grant had feared he would never recover. But he had, and he'd learned from his losses. He'd learned how to avoid ever again experiencing that pain. And now? How could he bear it if Emily left? That would be worse—incalculably worse—than Mickey's leaving.

Grant closed his eyes, and for an instant he was back in Chicago, watching Mickey being forced into the carriage, wailing as if his heart were being torn from his body. That was what it had felt like to Grant, seeing his only friend leaving and knowing he was powerless to stop it.

Powerless.

The word hit him with the force of a speeding locomotive, destroying the barriers he had so carefully erected. Years of defenses crumbled under the onslaught of a single word. Power. That was the difference. Grant's eyes flew open. Of course! The truth had been there all along. He had simply been unable to see it. He had been mired in the past, never recognizing how much he had changed and that he was no longer the same Grant Randall who had had his friends wrenched from him. Emily had tried to tell him that, but he hadn't listened. He had been too trapped by his fears, too caught in the pattern of believing that life held only heartache in store for him. It had taken Jeanne-Claude's prodding to make him realize how much was at stake.

Grant knew what he had to do. If he had enough courage, he would put the past behind him and make his own future.

He accepted the fact that he could not have stopped Mickey from leaving, any more than he could have prevented Mrs. Schiller from taking Augustus to the pound. He had been a young boy then; he had indeed been powerless. But he was a child no longer. This time it could be different. This time Grant could fight for what he loved. He could confront his fears and conquer them. And this time, if he was very, very lucky, there could be one of those happy endings that Emily believed in.

Grant grabbed his hat and opened the door. "I've got to go," he told Jeanne-Claude.

"You're the most stubborn person I've ever met." Emily glared at her brother. It didn't matter that he couldn't see her; she knew that her tone reflected her expression.

"That's what Jeanne-Claude says." Theo reached back to steady himself against the chair, then sat down again. Emily took it as a good sign. At least he was no longer trying to evict her from his room.

"Then Jeanne-Claude's a wise woman. I think I'll like having her for a sister-in-law."

A flush rose to Theo's cheeks. It was another good sign. "Don't be absurd," he said. "You can't have a sister-in-law unless I have a wife."

Emily leaned forward and laid her hand on her brother's. "You'd have a wife if you'd stop being so stubborn." This was one argument he wasn't going to win.

Theo's face mirrored his annoyance, and he snatched his hand away as if Emily's touch burned him. It was, she knew, her words rather than her touch that irritated Theo. He never had liked being told he was wrong. "I'm getting tired of that refrain," he groused.

"Then admit that I'm right, and I'll stop repeating it."

"You're not right."

"Yes, I am. If Jeanne-Claude loves you—and I think she does—your blindness won't matter."

A flicker of hope crossed Theo's face, then disappeared. "I can't burden her that way." Though his words were harsh, Emily thought she heard a wistful note in them. The man loved Jeanne-Claude. There was no doubt about that. He was simply too stubborn to admit it.

"I'm getting tired of that refrain." Emily threw Theo's words back at him. "Now, listen to me. No interruptions." She glared at her brother again, as he started to open his mouth. Though he could not see her, he closed it again. Emily grinned, realizing that although many things had changed, her twin could still gauge her moods.

"I told you about Beau," she said, "and how he was hurt. Do you think I love him any less because he may always walk with a limp?"

Theo shook his head impatiently. "That's different."

"It's not. Love is love." Theo snorted, his disagreement obvious, and Emily considered what she'd said. "Maybe you're right," she agreed. "Maybe it is different. Love between a man and a woman should be stronger than love for a dog. But that doesn't make what I said any less true. It's all the more reason for you to ask Jeanne-Claude to marry you."

Theo's face was set in the stubborn expression Emily had seen so many times. She had to do something to jolt him out of his mistaken beliefs. So much was at stake. His happiness, Jeanne-Claude's, perhaps even Emily's own. "Are you going to spend the rest of your life alone," she demanded, "simply because you were too cowardly to propose to the woman you love?"

The blood drained from Theo's face, then rushed back. "I'm not a coward," he declared.

Emily wasn't going to let him continue to lie to himself. "That's what it looks like from here."

Theo leaned forward, closing the gap between them. Though his eyes were bandaged, there was no ignoring the fierceness of his expression. "Words are cheap, little sister. Actions cost more." He reached out, fumbling a little as he gripped Emily's chin. "Let's turn this around. Why don't you tell me what you're going to do about Grant?"

Emily started to squirm, but Theo held her firmly. "Don't tell me Grant's just a friend," her brother continued. "Remember, I've known you your whole life. You can't fool me any more than I can fool you." Theo stroked Emily's cheek. "I hear the smile in your voice when you say his name, and I heard the way your breath caught when I asked you about him. Face it, Emily. You love the man."

She couldn't deny it. She didn't even want to.

Emily had thought that when she found love, it would announce itself like the brass band that marched down Main Street each Independence Day. She had expected it to be sudden and filled with fanfare. Instead, love had been like a spring flower, almost unnoticed when it first emerged from the ground. But, like a flower, it had grown steadily, and now that it was in full bloom, it was dazzling in its beauty.

"I do love Grant," she told her brother. "And if he'll have me, I'm going to marry him." Even though it wasn't conventional, Emily suspected she would have to propose to Grant, for the man's fear of commitment was so strong that she doubted he would ever take the first step. But that wasn't going to stop her. She loved him, and she was going to fight for that love.

"What about you?" she asked Theo. "What are you going to do? Are you going to let me be the only brave one in this family?"

Theo was silent for a long moment, and Emily saw the indecision on his face. Though different in origin, her brother's fears were as strong as Grant's. At last Theo grinned. "It pains me to admit this, but you're right, Sis. The Wentworth twins are in love. Let's go for it. Let's catch the brass ring."

Chapter Thirteen

"Where is he?" Emily looked around the room, feeling as if she'd walked onto the stage of a play where the characters were frozen in place. Jeanne-Claude sat at the table where she'd been when Emily first entered her brother's room. Beau lay on the floor, raising his head slightly when Emily came out. Only one player was gone: the most important one. Grant's cup sat on the table, the sole sign that he'd once been there.

Jeanne-Claude shrugged. "I don't know." Though she did not meet Emily's gaze, her words sounded sincere. There would be no reason for her to lie. "He grabbed his hat and left without saying where he was going. Then I heard the car."

"The car?" Emily glanced outside. Hortense was indeed gone. How had she not heard the distinctive sound of the motor? The only reason Emily could imagine was that she had been so focused on her discussion with her brother that she had blocked all other thoughts. She hadn't wanted to think about Grant, and so she hadn't heard him leave.

"Grant's not supposed to drive a car," Emily said, still trying to accept the fact that he was gone and that he had taken the car. This was no casual drive, she knew. Grant must have left Maillochauds. "His eyesight's not good enough." Why hadn't he waited? She would have driven him wherever he wanted to go.

Jeanne-Claude shrugged again, and this time she smiled at Emily as she said, "When a man gets an idea in his head, he won't let anything stand in his way." As her gaze flitted to Theo's door, Emily realized that the Frenchwoman was speaking not only of Grant. "All he said was that he had to go."

"I see." And Emily did. If she hadn't been such a fool— as blind as her brother—she would have realized that this would happen. Grant had given her ample warning. Their agreement had been that he would accompany her to Maillochauds. Not once had he promised anything more. Not once had he spoken of anything further in the future than Emily's reunion with her brother. She had known that her life and Grant's would diverge, just as hers and Theo's had. Grant's leaving should not have been a surprise. It should not have hurt. But it did. Oh, it did.

Beau struggled to his feet and licked Emily's hand. "At least he left you," she said, stroking the dog's head. Emily forced a smile onto her face. There was no reason to inflict her mood on anyone else. "We'll be going now," she told Jeanne-Claude. "Theo needs to talk to you." And if her brother did what he had promised, there'd be a happy ending for one of the Wentworth twins.

Though the light in Jeanne-Claude's eyes told Emily how much the lovely Frenchwoman wanted to be with Theo, Jeanne-Claude rose and walked to the door with Emily. "Let me give you the wagon," she said. "I told Grant we had no need of it, and Beau could use it."

Though Beau protested being put into the wagon, Emily was grateful for the gift. The dog was not ready to walk the whole distance into the center of the town, and she was not certain she could carry him that far.

Emily started toward town, then turned around. Eventually she would have to go back. She couldn't leave Maillochauds without saying good-bye to Theo and making sure that he had kept his word. She wouldn't tell him that Grant had left before she could ask him to marry her. Besides, there were belongings to collect, and transportation to arrange. With Hortense gone, Emily would have to find another way to return to Calais. All that would come later. Now she needed time to think.

Emily looked at the sky, her smile ironic as she realized that the day matched her mood. The beautiful blue sky and puffy clouds that had lifted her spirits early that morning were gone, replaced by a sullen sky that smelled of rain. So, too, had her optimism disappeared. All that was left was a future that seemed as bleak as the day.

How on earth could she bear a future without Grant? Beau whimpered, and Emily rubbed his head. "We'd better get used to it," she told him. "It looks like it's just the two of us from now on." She bit the inside of her mouth, wishing she hadn't spoken. Hearing her fears voiced made them seem all too real. Perhaps if she whistled. But though she puckered her lips, no sounds emerged. It appeared that whistling was another thing she could not do without Grant.

Emily shuddered as she turned off the road, following a footpath through the fields. Though artillery fire had scorched the ground in huge patches, the first brave shoots of grass had begun to appear. The earth, it appeared, was more resilient than the human heart. For Emily was certain that the horrible emptiness deep inside her would never be filled. Tennyson might claim that it was 'better to have loved and lost than never to have loved at all,' but he was wrong, so very, very wrong. No one should have to endure this kind of pain.

Emily stopped to pick up a branch. Though Beau could not yet run to fetch a stick, he might enjoy chewing on it. "It's all right, boy," she said. Perhaps if she convinced the dog, she might be able to convince herself that they would survive without Grant.

This was what Grant had feared, the pain of losing someone he loved. Emily took a deep breath, trying to quell the tremors that wracked her. She had thought she had understood Grant's fears, but she had not. The reality was far worse than she had dreamed possible. Not even in her worst nightmares had she known a pain this deep, nor had she guessed that the hole Grant's departure had left inside her would be so large. How had he survived losing more than one person? No wonder he had encased his heart in armor. No wonder he was so afraid of loving. Keeping his distance was the only way he could ensure that there would be no more pain.

Emily slowed the wagon as she descended a small hill. She couldn't risk having Beau tumble out and injure his leg again. The dog was all she had left.

She couldn't blame Grant for leaving. After all, he had broken no promises. His agreement had been to help Emily get to Maillochauds, and he had done that. Grant had never promised that he would stay, once she was reunited with Theo. She shouldn't have expected anything more. But why, oh why, had he not said good-bye? Surely he could have done that. Leaving without a word seemed so cruel, almost heartless. If she had been the one leaving, she would have . . .

Emily stopped, unsure what she would have done. Perhaps Grant had left the way he did to protect himself. She knew he feared commitment and that he was a master at erecting protective shields. Perhaps his abrupt departure was yet another shield. Perhaps Grant could not bear the thought of saying good-bye, any more than she could imagine herself saying those words to him.

As Beau barked at a butterfly, Emily ruffled his fur. "We'll be fine, Beau. You and I are survivors." But the words sounded as hollow as she felt.

She had thought Grant loved her. Admittedly, he had never said the words, but he had shown that he cared for her in so many ways. There were the smiles that could only be called tender, the touches that set her blood to boiling. And then there was his kiss. How could she forget that and the way it had made her feel beautiful and cherished and, yes, loved? Grant loved her. She was confident of that. She wasn't wrong about that; she had not mistaken his feelings.

The problem came later. Emily had believed that Grant's love was strong enough to overcome his fears. That was where she had been wrong. Whatever he felt for her wasn't as strong as his fears. That was why he had turned away when she had told him she loved him. He had feared that she would be like Carl and Mickey and Augustus. Grant had been afraid that she would leave. And, because he couldn't bear to have another person leave him, Grant had done the only thing he could to protect his heart. He had been the one to leave.

With that realization came the even more painful one that it was her fault. If she had been wiser, Grant might not have left. He had given her a weapon to fight her own fears. He had taught her to whistle in the dark. Emily could have given him an even more powerful weapon, and yet she had not. Though she had told Grant she loved him, she had not convinced him that the love was so strong that nothing on earth could make her leave him and forfeit it.

Emily had told Theo that love was the most important gift one person could give another. She believed that. She had not the slightest doubt that what she felt for Grant was love and that the love would endure, but though she was certain, she had not convinced Grant. And because she had not, he had been unarmed in the battle against fear. A soldier should not go into battle unprepared, but Grant had. As a result, they had both lost. It was over now, the final battle of the war.

Emily stared into the distance, trying to make sense of the emptiness that surrounded her. What would she do with the rest of her life? The threat of rain was closer now. She ought to turn back and try to reach shelter before the torrents began. But Emily did not move. Instead, as she watched the rain clouds gather, a kaleidoscope of memories flashed before her. The times she and Grant had run from a shop, dodging raindrops. The times she'd had to repair the car in the rain, when Grant had stood next to her, holding an umbrella over her in a vain attempt to keep them both dry. The day they'd taken shelter in an abandoned barn and found Beau. They had laughed at the rain. They had cursed it. But most of all, they had been together in it. For the rest of her life, Emily knew that whenever it rained, she would think of Grant.

She laughed, but there was no mirth in the sound. It wasn't only rain that triggered thoughts of him. Even if she moved to a desert without a drop of water, she would not escape memories of Grant. He was part of her life, and he always would be.

"Time to return," Emily said to Beau as she turned the wagon and headed toward Maillochauds. She couldn't run away from her memories. All she could do was set a course for the future. She would take Beau back to Calais with her, and once they arrived, she would be the best ambulance driver in all of France. She would do everything she could to help the men who'd been wounded in this awful war. And, if she had wounds of her own, she wouldn't let anyone see them.

Emily would joke with the men; she would avoid every

rut in the road; she would keep the ambulance in perfect condition. The one thing she would not do was read a single Grant Randall column. It was one thing to endure pain; it was another to deliberately inflict it. She had dreamed of a future with Grant. Now she knew that those dreams would never come true. Instead, Emily would be like Mme. Vigny, cherishing the memories of the time she had spent with her loved one.

Beau pricked his ears and tipped his head to one side, as if he heard something. "What is it, Beau?" The dog yipped and strained forward. "I'm sorry, boy, but you're not ready to chase rabbits." Grant had said . . . Emily clenched her teeth as a fresh wave of pain washed over her.

Beau yipped again, and his tail began to thump against the wagon's side. Something was exciting the dog. Seconds later, Emily felt her heart lurch. There was no doubt about it. The sound Beau heard was Hortense's motor.

Perhaps Grant was simply driving by on his way to his next destination. But when the engine stopped, Emily's heart began to race. Grant had come back! He wasn't going to leave without saying good-bye! She quickened her pace as she climbed the small rise, wishing she weren't pulling the wagon but knowing she would never leave Beau behind. Being abandoned would hurt him almost as much as Grant's leaving had hurt her.

When she reached the top of the hill, Emily saw Grant. He was walking toward her, and his lips were pursed as if he were whistling. Emily's heart skipped another beat as she realized this was only the second time Grant had voluntarily admitted that he was afraid. What did he fear? Could it possibly be the same thing Emily dreaded—being separated from the person she loved, the one she had dreamed would share the rest of her life with her?

Whatever it was Grant feared, Emily wanted to help him. It was clear that he was fighting his fears the only way he knew. She could give him more powerful weapons. This was her chance. Before Grant left, she would tell him of her love. He might reject it—that was a risk she had to take—but she would make certain that this time he understood just how much Emily loved him and that she would never leave him.

Beau was not waiting. He jumped out of the wagon, then hobbled toward Grant as fast as he could. Though Grant bent down to ruffle the dog's fur, he kept his eyes on Emily. "Emily," he said, and there was a note in his voice that she had never before heard.

Unencumbered by the wagon, Emily hurried toward the man she loved. "I'm glad you came back," she said. "There's something I need to tell you before you leave." In the distance, thunder rumbled. Rain was imminent, but Emily didn't care. All that mattered was that Grant was here. She still had a chance.

He shook his head and laid a finger across her lips. "Later. There'll be time later." Grant dropped his hand, as if conscious that the gesture was too familiar for a public place.

Emily wasn't certain there would be a later. "I thought you were in a hurry to get to Paris or wherever it is you were going."

"What made you think that?"

"You drove Hortense."

Grant's smile was wry. "That I did, but not very well, I'm afraid. The only reason I risked damaging the car and myself was that it would have taken too long to walk." Behind his spectacles, his eyes sparkled with mirth. "You're right. I was in a hurry."

Beau settled on the grass next to Grant, his brown eyes fixed on the man who had convinced an over-worked Army physician to save a dog's leg. In Beau's eyes, Grant was a hero. Emily didn't disagree. Grant's actions had been heroic, but it went deeper than that. If Emily had been writing a fairytale, Grant would have been the hero, the one who shared a life of happily-ever-after with the lady he had rescued.

"Of course," Grant said with another self-deprecating smile, "I'd forgotten how long it would take to get an answer."

"An answer?" For a man who made his living crafting words, he wasn't making a lot of sense.

"I telegraphed my editor asking for a two-week leave."

"Two weeks?" Emily felt as if she were extracting information from one of the most taciturn men on earth, not from Grant Randall, wordsmith *extraordinaire*. To her knowledge, he had never taken a holiday. Why was he doing it now? And why wouldn't he let her tell him what was foremost in her mind? She couldn't—and she wouldn't—let him leave again without knowing just how strong and enduring her love was. She couldn't let him leave without trying to heal some of the wounds that had been inflicted so many years ago.

"I would have asked for more," Grant said, as if that explained everything, "but I knew he'd never agree. It's not as long as I'd like for a honeymoon, but . . ."

"Honeymoon?" Emily stared at Grant, not believing she'd heard him correctly. Honeymoon! Grant, the man who had once told her he had an 'unfortunate habit' of becoming attached to people, was talking about a honeymoon. Though thunder rumbled again, Emily felt as if the day had suddenly turned beautiful and sunny.

Grant appeared almost sheepish. "It's not the way I imagined it. I would have liked moonlight and roses and a diamond ring. Instead . . ." He looked around and frowned. "It's a cloudy afternoon, the air smells of rain and war, it's too early for roses, and there was not a single ring to be found in Maillochauds." Grant reached for Emily's hands.

"All I have to offer you is my heart and enough love to last a lifetime."

The happiness that had started to well within her heart when Grant had pronounced the word 'honeymoon' now filled it to the top. The man Emily loved was saying the words she had longed to hear. Somehow, though she had once thought it impossible, her dreams were coming true.

"I don't need moonlight and roses and diamonds. Love is all I ever wanted," Emily said. She watched as a glimmer of hope lit Grant's eyes. Even now, he had not conquered all his fears. She had to convince him! "A lifetime of love is what I can offer you. That and the promise that I'll never leave you. Never."

Grant nodded slowly, the shadows seeming to recede from his eyes. "For years I thought that the worst thing that could happen to me would be to lose another person I loved. Today I realized I was wrong. There could be something even worse, and that would be to walk away from love. I love you, Emily, and I don't want to live without you."

Though the ground was still damp, Grant knelt at Emily's feet. "You know the worst about me. I can't see very well; I drive even worse than that; I'm afraid to take chances." Behind his spectacles, Grant's eyes were brimming with an emotion Emily had once only dreamed of seeing. The love that shone from them was the same love she knew he could see reflected in hers.

"I know that I'm not a knight in shining armor," Grant continued. "I may never be able to give you a fairytale castle, and I can't promise happily ever after. What I can promise you is that no one will ever love you more than I do." He took a deep breath, then exhaled. "Will you have me, flaws and all? Will you say the words that will make my life complete? Will you marry me, Emily Wentworth?"

Emily tugged on Grant's hands. When he was standing,

she leaned forward, pressing her lips to his. "Yes, my darling. I will!"

Three days later, the town of Maillochauds had its first double wedding.

Dear Reader,

I hope you enjoyed Emily's and Grant's story and that you're looking forward to Martha's tale. Tom Fleming, a celebrated photographer, comes to Canela on a cross-country search for 'The Fourth of July Woman,' a woman whose picture will inspire the men at the front, reminding them of all that's waiting for them at home. Tom is sure he's found the perfect woman when he sees Martha Wentworth. Unfortunately for Tom, Martha, who's still mourning her husband's death, is unwilling to be put on public display, even as part of the war effort. But life, as Tom has good reason to know, doesn't always go according to plan. Events conspire to throw him and Martha together, and—though she had not dreamed it possible—Martha's grief begins to ease as Tom teaches her to laugh at the thunder. The happy ending they both seek may never happen, though, for the war is being fought on many fronts, including the home front. Soon Martha's and Tom's new-found love is threatened by the same forces that divide her hometown.

I hope you'll join me for Martha and Tom's story, Laughing at the Thunder, *which should be available in mid 2004.*

If this is your first War Brides *Romance, you may have wondered about Emily's sister Carolyn, the Wentworth daughter who's cap over boots in love with her new husband. Even Emily doesn't know the whole story of how Carolyn met him and the obstacles she had to overcome before she found her happy ending.* Dancing in the Rain, *which tells Carolyn's story, is currently available.*

Happy reading,
Amanda Harte

8/04